A Free Land

<u>Chapter 1</u>

Charlottesville, Virginia, August 2017

It was one of the tensest days Toby had ever experienced in his many years on the police force. The fallout from the riots in Charlottesville was making national news. He and his partner, Roy Mason, were patrolling the area and everyone was on high alert in case more violence was to erupt. Fortunately it seemed like things were cooling down a bit, but everyone was on edge and you could feel the tension in the air.

Toby and Roy said very little to each other during work that day. It was like they had some type of unspoken agreement between them that in order to preserve their partnership they simply wouldn't discuss the events that had taken place. Being completely opposite in political views and background, they knew that there was no way they would ever agree on these issues.

While Toby knew that Roy did not have any real racial hatred in him, he nonetheless knew that certain topics they would never be able to understand from the same point of view. Toby was African-American and had grown up in an atmosphere and climate of racial hatred and fear that Roy would never understand as a white man growing up in the South. It was simply like living in two different worlds.

Their problem was that even though they had totally different views on the recent events, without even having to tell one another, they both had the same job – maintain public order and enforce the law, which these days was becoming increasingly difficult.

As they were on patrol around where the Confederate monuments were, they had to keep an eye out for any suspicious activity. The truth of the matter is that while Toby was very against vandalism of any kind, having had his own house vandalized on more than one occasion, deep down he felt that the people protesting to bring down the Confederate monuments were right in belief and ideals, if not in method.

Every time he would see one of those Confederate statues or

the Confederate flags proudly displayed around town, Toby felt a cringe. He would try to keep his feelings to himself as much as possible, when you're a police officer you have to repress a lot of unpleasant feelings in order to do your job, but seeing these flags and monuments celebrating a slave owning state filled him with a sense of loathing and fear. The Civil War was over 150 years ago and the losing side still has not accepted that they lost and that the war was truly over.

Roy had a different attitude. He came from a long line of prominent Southerners, or at least they had been prominent a few generations back. Roy proudly displayed images in his office and in his home of his ancestors, some of whom were high-ranking military officers in the Confederacy. He even had a Confederate flag dating from the Civil War that he proudly displayed in a glass case and considered it to be one of his most valuable possessions.

Toby could understand what it meant to him, and that it meant something entirely different, but to Toby it would still always be a symbol of slavery and racial hatred. There was simply no way around that. Taking pride in your heritage is one thing, taking pride in the wrong things in your heritage is another.

It was Toby's desperate hope that whatever happened today that it would be nothing that would inflame the tension that they were both trying to avoid, the uncomfortable topics that they did not want to discuss.

Fortunately, in contrast to the violence of the past week, this week was comparatively peaceful. Other than a few parking tickets and a few citations for graffiti they had had no major confrontations, none of the kind that resulted in violence. All standard police work, nothing to get excited about.

Both of them knew however that it couldn't last. As they were patrolling past a statue of Robert E Lee, a young African-American teenager was looking around as though he were watching for someone. Not aware that they were watching him, he picked up a large rock and threw it at the statue of Robert E Lee and hit it right between the eyes. Toby had to admit, the kid had good aim!

"We've got a delinquent vandalizing state property," Roy said.

As they pulled up the teenager stopped in his tracks, aware that he had been spotted.

Roy pulled over the police car and the two of them stepped out.

"What do you think you're doing there boy?" Roy asked. Toby always hated it when he referred to an African-American teenager as boy. Even though he was just a boy, he noticed that Roy never used that term when dealing with a white delinquent teenager.

"I wasn't doing anything," the teenager said as he looked down at his shoes, an indication of guilt, knowing that he had done something and that they had seen him.

"I believe that you just threw a rock at that statue," Roy said as he pointed to the statue of Robert E Lee.

"Is it a crime to throw a rock? I wasn't throwing it at a person." The teenager continued looking down at his shoes and kept scraping his feet across the pavement.

"You threw it at that statue, that statue is public property. I could have you booked on charges of vandalism."

"I didn't damage your crummy statue."

"Boy don't you respect history and heritage? Do you have any idea who that is?"

"Yeah I do, it's Robert E Lee. I ain't stupid."

Roy suddenly started feeling rather cocky and he smiled. "So you do know who it is, but do you know what he represents?"

"Yeah, he was a racist fuck who fought for slavery."

The smile disappeared from Roy's face. "Watch your language boy. That man fought for his country."

"He fought against his country. He was a traitor. He was fighting for slavery."

Roy shook his head in disapproval. "You know a lot of good people on both sides were killed in that war. It was an ugly time in our history, but that doesn't diminish the sacrifices made."

"Sacrifices! Robert E Lee was an asshole, so was anyone who followed him."

Now he had done it, Roy was getting mad.

"So are you calling my ancestors assholes?" Roy said as he lifted up the boy's chin. "I want you to look at me when you answer me boy."

"I don't know nothing about your ancestors."

"Would you desecrate a graveyard?"

"This ain't no graveyard."

"Roy, it was a minor offense," Toby spoke up, trying hard to remain silent during this whole confrontation. "I think we should let him off with a warning."

"The youth today, they have no respect," said Roy as he shook his head. "And this boy has delinquent written all over his face."

"Do you promise that if we let you off with a warning that we will not see you around here again?" Toby asked as he put his arm on the boy's shoulder and gave him a look that said you better realize that I am doing you a favor.

"I promise," the boy said in a whisper.

"What was that?" Roy asked.

"I said I promise," the boy said loudly as he looked at Roy, who still frowned at him.

"Get the hell out of here!" Roy shouted as he shooed the boy away. "And just be glad that I didn't think you were trying to harm anyone and shoot you."

"Roy," Toby said, now angry at the suggestion that Roy would shoot an unarmed African-American teenager and was deliberately using that to scare the boy.

"You know I wouldn't shoot him," Roy said. "But if I give him a good scare he won't do it again in the future."

The two of them got back into the police car and both of them could feel the tension in the air thickening. But Roy wasn't going to hold back any longer.

"These kids today, they just have no respect for heritage," Roy said. "Nobody has respect for country anymore. You got people vandalizing statues, football players refusing to stand for the national anthem and the whole country going to hell."

"You didn't have to threaten that child like that," Toby said, interrupting Roy before he continued with his rant.

"These kids have to learn respect. We are raising an entire generation of anarchists with no respect for the flag, no respect for authority, no appreciation of heritage. The sooner they learn this, the better."

"Threatening to shoot him, especially given how many boys like him have been shot unnecessarily, that was just downright mean."

"You ask me it should be a major crime to desecrate a flag or a monument like that. We really shouldn't have just let him off with a warning. Maybe I shouldn't have threatened to shoot him, I mean I think he knows that I was kidding around, but we should have booked him for something. We let him get away with this I guarantee he will probably be back at the first opportunity to cause mischief again. If we raised these kids to stand at attention and salute the flag at the drop of a hat I can guarantee we wouldn't be having all this crime and violence and poverty. Now if we want to make America great again we have to go back to the way things were in the olden days, when people had respect for authority, an appreciation of heritage and respect for the flag. We lost that and look at what it has gotten us. They should force those NFL players to stand for the flag, that isn't what this country is about."

"Actually that is what this country was about. This country was founded on the freedom to not have to salute a flag or bow before a statue or fear for their lives if they stage a protest. That's what distinguishes this country from a totalitarian regime. The flag is just a meaningless symbol."

"But how could you think like that, you're a police officer for Christ's sake. You're putting your life on the line risking your ass every day protecting and serving the public and this is the kind of disrespect we have to put up with. These kids just have nothing better to do. It's just an absolute disgrace that people won't stand for the national anthem anymore."

"It's a disgrace that people are more upset about that than the thing that they were protesting."

"Protesting what, the fact that they live in a country so free that they can make millions of dollars and disrespect their flag as much as they want."

"Protesting a nation where people like us get away with murder of innocents just because of the color of their skin."

"Here we go again, bringing race into it. How many black teenagers have you seen me shoot in the head? I can tell you that in all my years on the force I have never fired my gun upon a suspect. I have drawn my gun before, I've threatened to use it, but I have never shot someone, and for that I am very glad."

"That's not the point. Just because we have not shot anyone in the head, if we don't stand up against those that do this unjustly, then we are disgracing our own profession. It is the job of the good cops to keep the bad ones in line. If we don't do that we have no right to call ourselves the good cops. Haven't you ever heard the phrase who will police the police?"

Roy shook his head. "We are just never going to agree on this are we?"

"I guess not," said Toby. "I guess we will just have to agree to disagree."

Roy was going to say something more, but he realized that he would only make the situation worse. They had gotten into some pretty heated arguments before but they always tried to resolve them amicably. They knew when they weren't going to agree that it was best to just drop the issue.

Fortunately the rest of the day, while they were rather quiet and didn't have much friendly banter, was uneventful and free of any type of other major incidents. Just another day of handing out parking tickets and patrolling around looking for trouble that they were fortunate enough not to find.

At the end of the day they departed peacefully and wished each other a good night and said that they would see each other tomorrow. Tomorrow, after all, was another day, and they both desperately hoped in their heart of hearts that it would be a better one.

Chapter 2

Roy went home that night feeling especially exhausted from the tense day he had. As soon as he walked in the door from the evening shift his wife Charlotte looked up at him.

"Rough day at work?" Charlotte asked as she kissed him.

"You don't know the half of it," Roy said as he began

changing out of his uniform.

"Do you want to talk about it?"

"Not really."

"Are you sure?"

"There are some things you can only understand from being a police officer."

"Was it some type of tense moment between you and Toby?"

Roy nodded. "Again though, I don't really want to talk about it. I think I just want to get right to sleep."

"Don't worry dear; I am sure that tomorrow will be a better day." She kissed him again as he got undressed and got into bed.

As he slowly drifted off to sleep couldn't help but feeling extremely restless and maybe even a bit dizzy, but eventually he managed to fall into a fitful sleep while staring at the framed Confederate flag of his grandfather right across from his bed.

The next morning he woke up to feel the sun warming his body. Despite not sleeping great, he did feel more refreshed than he thought he would under the circumstances. Just from feeling the sun on his face he knew that today was going to be another scorcher.

As he woke up he realized that Charlotte had already woken up and he figured that she had probably started making breakfast for him.

As he walked down the hall he couldn't help but feel something was rather different. That was when he realized the obvious, his house did look different. In fact his house was much nicer than it had looked when he went to sleep last night.

He walked into the kitchen to find that Charlotte had already made a huge stack of pancakes and that his children Atticus and Bonnie were already gobbling them down.

"Good morning dear," said Charlotte as she placed down a huge stack of pancakes in front of him. "Did you sleep well last night?"

"I slept okay, but I have to ask the obvious question."

"And what would that be?" Charlotte asked with a smile followed by a puzzled look.

"I am talking about all these new appliances and furniture!" Roy shouted. "Since when do we have a big screen TV in the living room and all these fancy antiques?"

Charlotte looked at him like he was crazy. "What are you talking about dear? We have always had these."

"Really, I hadn't noticed! Did you make over the entire house while I was asleep?"

"I really do not know what you are talking about."

"I am talking about the fact that you seemingly went on a shopping spree last night without telling me and bought a bunch of extremely expensive appliances and antiques that we quite simply can't afford. I know that my job certainly doesn't pay enough, and your job certainly doesn't pay enough."

"My job?" Charlotte said as she began to laugh and waved her hand dismissively. "What job?"

"What job?! Did you quit your job as a secretary?"

"Is this some type of a joke? I've never had a job. Since when does a proper Southern woman like me have a job?"

"Since always! Since we realized that we could not afford to live on a single income. Police officers aren't millionaires, in case you haven't noticed!"

That was when Roy looked at the clock to see that he had woken up late. "Speaking of work, I really have to get going. But we are going to talk about this when we get home, believe me."

As Roy walked out into his front porch he noticed that the familiar American flag was not waving, but in its place was hanging a large Confederate flag. When did Charlotte put that up he wondered? But he didn't have time to worry about that now; he had to go to work.

As he looked in the driveway he saw what looked like a brand-new car, which caused him to do a double take. "Charlotte!" he shouted at which point she came running out.

"What's the matter dear?" she said smiling.

"Where the hell is my car?!"

"What are you talking about, it's right there," she said pointing to the sleek new red car in the driveway.

"This is not my car. I could never afford a car like this on my salary. What the hell is going on here Charlotte? I'm serious now, I'm not joking anymore."

Charlotte came up to Roy and felt his head. "You don't have a fever. Are you sure you are okay?"

Roy pushed her away and looked over the sleek red car in front of him and felt it with his own two hands. It truly was a magnificent car, one that he figured he would never be able to afford in a million years. He looked around back to the license plate to see that the license plate had a Confederate flag on it as well and a different license plate number than what he had remembered.

"Charlotte is this car stolen?" he said as he got up in her face to which she looked very nervous.

"Roy you are scaring me."

"No, you're the one scaring me! Where on earth did this car come from?"

"It's your car, you've had it for like a year or two now, although you keep it in such good shape that it looks brand-new doesn't it? Maybe if you get your promotion we can get an even nicer one."

Roy felt in his pocket and took out his keys and found that it fit inside of the car perfectly and the door opened. He immediately looked in the glove compartment to find his license and registration and found was all in order.

Charlotte came over to him and smiled. "Shouldn't you be getting to work? I want to get back inside, it's too hot out to be outside today."

"Well then why are you dressed like that," he said as it suddenly occurred to him that Charlotte was wearing a long dress. She pretty much always wore either a skirt or pants. "Why don't you just put on your jeans?"

"Me, put on pants?!" she said as she began laughing.

"What's so funny?"

"Are you suggesting that I dress like some type of a whore? It would be downright indecent."

Roy began rubbing his forehead and looked again at his watch. "I had better get to work, only when get home I think that we are going to have a really long chat about a whole great many things."

Charlotte smiled and kissed him. "Whatever you say dear,

have a good day at work."

As Roy drove to work the familiar route looked rather different. There had always been Confederate flags throughout the town, but never this many. He also saw a large billboard with a black man in chains that said "slaves obey your masters, it's the law."

"Well that's in poor taste," he said as he looked at the billboard. "I don't remember that being there the other day."

Roy was beginning to feel even more uncomfortable by the minute. Something was definitely not right here. He thought that he would relax himself by turning to the rock 'n roll station.

"In latest news," the radio said. "Another slave uprising took place in Northern Virginia and it took federal troops hours to put down. Over 155 Negroes were killed in the shootout. It is one of the worst racial uprisings that we have had all year and the governor says that these are growing worse and becoming a national epidemic."

Roy was so busy listening to the radio broadcast he didn't notice that cars were beeping at him to get moving so he turned off the radio and decided to continue driving to work, even though something was clearly not right.

Within a short time he arrived at the station and checked in.

"You're late Roy," said his boss, Mr. McGlocklin, as he was busy briefing the entire staff. "As you all no doubt have heard by now there was another slave uprising not very far from here, so we are to be on high alert today. If you see anything suspicious do not hesitate to bring people in. The governor has called for a curfew where all Negroes are to stay off the streets while we take care of this latest uprising. If you see any darker skinned person walking about stop them and check their papers or tattoos as they might be part of the rebellion. Does everybody understand?"

Roy raised his hand and Mr. McGlocklin pointed to him. "Roy, you have a question?"

"Yeah I have a question, what the fuck are you talking about?"

"Do you have a specific question or did you just come here to sass me?"

"Well first off where the hell is Toby?"

"Who the hell is Toby? Listen, we don't have time to play 20 questions, the entire state is on high alert and we need all units on patrol right away. You just get in the car with Buford and be on close look out for any suspicious looking niggers."

Roy looked around the office and suddenly noticed that it also did not look exactly the same. For one thing there was no sign of the American flag, only the Confederate one. There was also a picture on the wall of what seemed to be the president, but it wasn't president Trump, it was a person that he had never seen before named president Clifton. He also noticed that there were no African-Americans anywhere in the office, nor any women.

"Hey, are you ready?" Buford asked. "I swear sometimes you can be as lazy as a nigger."

"I don't think it's okay for you to be using that word," Roy said suddenly feeling intensely uncomfortable.

Buford burst out laughing and slapped Roy on the back. "You're rich man, really rich. The biggest nigger catcher in the entire county and you say not to use that word. You're funny; I've always said that about you, you have a very good rich sense of humor. Now come on let's get our asses on patrol, I think we're gonna have some action today, get to beat some nigger ass."

Roy was suddenly feeling like he was about to be sick so he ran to the bathrooms to see that there were two bathroom doors, a colored and a white bathroom. He went into the white bathroom and quickly used the toilet and then washed his face and looked in the mirror. That was the first time that he had taken a good look at his uniform to realize that it also looked different. He looked to see that he had a patch with the Confederate flag on it as well.

He reached into his pocket and took out his wallet. He looked at some of the money but he didn't see any sign of Abraham Lincoln. But what he did see were images of Robert E Lee and Jefferson Davis. He then took out his ID and found that he had a particular license that he didn't realize before. In addition to his badge he noticed that he had a special ID that said licensed bounty hunter and slave catcher general.

After seeing that he put everything back in his pockets, ran over to the toilet and began getting sick, because something was definitely not right here, and he hadn't the slightest idea what was going on. Whatever was going on he didn't like it, he really didn't like it.

Chapter 3

Roy was now beginning to feel somewhat faint. What the hell was happening? He must be hallucinating or something like that. Maybe it was heatstroke or he had been working too hard.

"Hey what's going on in there?" Buford said as he knocked on the door. "Are you okay?"

"Yeah I'm just feeling a little bit under the weather," said Roy as he composed himself.

"Well hurry up, we have a busy day ahead of us."

Roy got in the police car with Buford and said that maybe it was better if Buford drove today.

"Are you sure you're okay?" Buford said. "You're acting kind of strange today."

"What the hell is wrong with this world?" Roy said as he shook his head and wiped away some sweat.

"My thoughts exactly!" Buford said with a big laugh. "Back when I was a kid most of the niggers knew their place but now it seems like we have a new uprising practically every week. You can't even go out on the streets at night without fearing that you're going to be raped or assaulted by some type of escaped slave. I just hope that president Clifton cracks down on all of these degenerate Negroes. I voted for him last time but in all honesty despite the fact that he talks a big game I think that he is soft on the slave issue. I mean I have no doubt that he upholds slavery, but I don't think he realizes how under threat the institution has become. It really is sad to see our once proud nation going backwards like this, know what I mean?"

"You don't know the half of it, although I think I might be thinking of things in the different way than you are."

Buford laughed again. "I fully understand. I know that not everyone is as extreme in their anti-Negro stance as you are, but then you are the slave catcher general, no one has to deal with more niggers than you do on a daily basis. Luckily it doesn't seem like any of them are out now. Maybe the governor's warning put the fear of God into them, the heathen savages. I mean we bring these people here from savagery in Africa and try to civilize them and make useful workers out of them, but they are just so close to the level of animals that you just really can't control them. It's like our Nazi allies say, the black man is really closer to apes than to humans, so having a Negro slave is pretty much like having a very unruly pet, like a maybe somewhat bright cat or dog, but you don't forget that there is still a vicious animal that needs to be tightly controlled if you don't want them to rape and murder your families."

"Do you think maybe we can talk about something else?" Roy said as he felt his stomach turn.

"I understand, I don't need to tell you twice about the threat that uncontrolled Negroes and escaped slaves pose to the country, it's your job to take care of that. I always wanted to go into slave catching myself, but I think it's better to be an ordinary police officer. It's bad enough having to deal with those people all the time, although again I'm not sure if I would quite call them people."

"Do you know what, let's not talk about anything. Let's just enjoy some music. Why don't you put the rock 'n roll station on?"

"The what and what station?"

"Never mind."

"I'll put on some good music," said Buford as he turned on the radio and suddenly all sorts of loud banjo music came on.

"What the hell is this?"

"It's the latest hit song from the Banjo Brothers. A lot of people think it's kind of decadent because some people say it's very close to Negro music, which we of course know is totally illegal, and a good thing too because we have to protect the public decency, but I think that this is just some nice string music. Really calms the nerves in these troubled times that we live in."

"Whatever," said Roy as he was trying to distract himself. He must be having some type of really bad really freaky dream. He must have been suffering from heat stroke or that he ate something bad or that his argument with Toby was just making his sleep really restless. No way could this possibly be real.

"We have an 841 in progress," the police radio said. "All

officers proceed to 18th Street."

"What's an 841?"

"What's an 841?! Are you losing your memory as well?"

"I'm a bit under the weather remember, humor me."

"An unlawful gathering of Negroes in defiance of the governor's orders, oh I hope they resist, my baton needs to do some beating today."

Roy wanted to bail right out of the car right away but he didn't know how he would explain that. He just closed his eyes and wished hard that he would wake up but every time he opened his eyes he would see the same thing; streets lined with Confederate flags, and a pretty much all white population.

That was until they got to the scene of the alert where they could already see that they were some of the first ones there but a couple of other police cars were already outside of a small apartment building.

"What's going on?" Buford said as the two of them got out of the car.

"It seems it's a couple of the escaped slaves," the other officer on duty said as he pointed to the apartment. "They've barricaded themselves inside that apartment and they are taking hostages. We're going to send in some teargas to try and gas them out. Hopefully that will get them out without harming the hostages too much. Be on your ready when they come out. We have the dogs ready; we have the fire hoses ready, just have your guns drawn but try not to damage the goods. A dead slave isn't going to bring any money in and we would have to deal with the fallout of having destroyed private property, which would be a total PR nightmare."

As they began firing teargas into the apartment windows they trained their weapons on the door. First a couple of white people came running out screaming into the arms of the police. Then they saw an African-American man trying to run away and they knocked him to the floor with a hose.

"Sick the dogs on him!" Buford said. "Bite that nigger's balls off!"

"Don't damage the property!" the chief officer said as Roy reluctantly ran after Buford as they went up to man being pressed up against the wall by the force of the hose. As soon as they turned the hose off he fell to the floor and Buford drew his gun and pointed at him.

"Get up very slowly boy," Buford said as the man very slowly got up and put his arms behind his head. "Scan them Roy."

"Scan them?" Roy asked, suddenly baffled at what Buford was asking.

"Yeah, take out your scanner and scan his tattoo," Buford said as he put handcuffs on the man and exposed his arm which had a barcode on it. Roy reluctantly took out a scanning device and ran it over the barcode on the man's arm.

Roy looked at the computer monitor and suddenly a picture of the man came up as Jefferson. It listed him as having been missing from his master for several days now and there was a high reward for his return.

"All right, it looks like we're going to get a good bonus for this nigger," Buford said. "And since we managed to get him undamaged the reward should be even bigger. You're going back to your master boy, and man is he going to beat the hell out of you. I wish that I had the pleasure of doing so, but I don't want to damage the property, as much as I would really like to."

They scanned and processed Jefferson, then several others came running out of the building and were promptly arrested. One of them resisted and a police officer took out a stun gun and shocked him and then started kicking him on the ground.

"Hey don't hurt him!" Roy said as he ran over to that officer.

"He was resisting," the officer said. "You have to take a firm hand with them. Besides it's probably nothing compared to the beating that he is going to get when we bring him back to his master. You can tell from all the scars all over his body that this is a highly disobedient slave." The officer scanned him. "Yep, it looks like he has a history of escape. I think that with people like him it would probably be more cost-effective just to put him down, or maybe to harvest his body for organs, although I don't see what type of self-respecting white man would ever want the inferior organs of a nigger inside of them, but I guess it was a choice between that and death there isn't much of a choice, not that would be much of a life either.

You can't be a fully pure person if you have Negro parts in you. It's like being marked, like you carry their African disease in yourself or something. I've even heard those who have nigger parts inside of them are more prone to crime."

As all of the African-American men inside of the building were wrestled to the ground, handcuffed and scanned they saw what looked like a police paddy wagon arriving but with a particular design on the side that showed black men behind bars and that said slave patrol painted underneath.

"This was a good round up!" the chief officer in charge of operation said. "Nice and orderly and we managed to capture all of the slaves without having to kill any of them. I think that you're all going to get commendations and bonuses for this. Give yourselves a round of applause men for once again defending decent God-fearing white Americans from the menace of Negro degeneracy."

Everyone clapped except Roy but when he realized that people were staring he started feebly clapping but wanted to be sick. Shortly after that they went back to the station where they wrote up a report.

"You know this is really not fair," said Roy as he looked at all of the African-Americans they had locked up in their prison detention center.

"I know," said Buford. "They really should charge the masters for these operations when their disobedient slaves cause a public mess like this. It's a lack of their own discipline that causes their slaves to run wild. It's not fair that the American taxpayer should have to pay to round up escaped slaves like that, even though we all get good bonuses out of it. President Clifton said that if he is reelected he's going to increase the fines to masters for destructions caused by their slaves, and I'm all in favor of that. Hey they can pay us with the fines, use it to pay our bonuses!" Buford gave Roy a hard pat on the shoulder. "So do you want to go out and get something to drink after work?"

Roy shook his head. "As much as I could really use a drink, I really think I should get home to my wife. I am feeling kind of under the weather still and I would really just like to get home and put this day behind me."

"Okay, hope you feel better. If it's any consolation just think of that big juicy bonus you are going to get from the slaves that we helped to apprehend today. You can put a couple new notches on your Negro catching belt."

Roy quickly got home and walked in the door to find his family eating dinner.

"Hi dear, how was work," said Charlotte as she ran up and kissed him. "Tough day?"

Roy began laughing. "Charlotte you do not know the half of it. I can't imagine anyone having a worse day than me today, I just can't imagine. If anyone had a worse day than me today, may God have mercy on his soul."

And without even so much as looking at his dinner, Roy ran into his room, collapsed on the bed and totally passed out.

<u>Chapter 4</u>

Toby woke up with a start the next morning as he felt a shock go through his body.

"What the hell?!" Toby shouted as he grabbed his neck to find that it had a collar around it.

"Rise and shine my niggers," a voice said as Toby looked around to see that he was in a small room with several beds and several other African-Americans all with collars around their necks.

"Where the hell am I?" Toby asked as he looked around.

"Is something the matter Toby?" said a white man as he came towards him holding a remote control.

"Who the hell are you?" Toby asked.

"I am your master and you will address me as such if you do not want to get another shock," the man said.

"My what? You know kidnapping is illegal and I am a police officer and –" Toby began saying before he fell to the ground as he was rocked by another violent shock.

"My my my boy, someone's going to have to learn you some manners," the white man said as he put his foot on Toby's stomach. "You know if you want to talk to me you had better address me by proper title of Master."

"I have no master!" Toby shouted only to find himself

convulsing from another shock.

"You are being especially difficult this morning Toby," the white man said. "Now you are to address me by my proper title of Master Jefferson or I will continue to shock you until you lose control of your bowels. I'd rather not do that because then that would just be more of a mess for the rest of the slaves to clean up and you don't want to delay them getting to their more important tasks, now do you?"

Toby was about to raise his fist in anger but he saw the man with his finger on the button and knew that if he attempted anything he would just get another shock that would cause him to fall to the ground yet again.

"Now if you are willing to be a good and obedient slave like you are supposed to be I will let you get up without having a shock," the man said. "Now you will slowly rise and address me by my proper name and title."

Toby very slowly got up still feeling dizzy and seeing spots from the shock and looked at the man. He stared him directly in the face and felt like spitting. Who did this man think he was? Clearly he was crazy to be kidnapping a police officer like this. But also clearly the man had him at his mercy so he would have to play it safe.

"Excuse me Mr. Jefferson but where am I," Toby asked.

"It is Master Jefferson to you," the man said as he fingered the remote control as he looked directly at Toby.

"Master Jefferson, if I may be so bold as to ask, but where am I?" Toby said.

"Boy is you trying to be funny with me?"

"No sir, master Sir. But what am I doing in this place?"

Mr. Jefferson laughed, with something of a snort. "You are here on in the governor's mansion and you are here to work like a good little slave. Now if you have had enough with the questions I suggest you get to work if you don't want to get a beating later. I have a busy day ahead of me. When you are running for president every day is a busy day and I can't have any of my niggers slacking off, got me?"

Toby was looking at him to see if he could perhaps grab that remote control and escape but he figured he had better keep playing it safe. Clearly whoever this lunatic was he was dangerously unstable and had a clear position of advantage over him.

"Yes master Jefferson," Toby said as he looked down at his toes.

"Good, now you get to work with the other slaves cleaning the house. I have important delegates visiting from our allies in the Third Reich who are coming to help me with my campaign for the presidency and I want to make a good impression on them. I don't want any disobedience or you will pay dearly for it, do you understand?"

"Yes master Jefferson," Toby said as he continued looking at his toes.

"That goes for all of you," Mr. Jefferson said.

"Yes master Jefferson," replied all of the slaves in unison.

"Good now get your lazy nigger asses to work," Mr. Jefferson said as he left the room.

"What the hell do you think you are doing standing up to the master like that?" another of the African-American men said as he walked up to Toby. "You trying to get us all a beating or a shock? Do you have a death wish?"

"I'm sorry, but you are?" Toby asked.

"Did you get amnesia or something?" the man asked. "It's me, George, your closest friend, who is wondering if his best friend has suddenly lost his mind."

"I might very well have amnesia or could be losing my mind. How the hell did I get here and what is this crazy place?"

"This is the governor's mansion," George said. "We are all master Jefferson's slaves."

"I am no man's slave," Toby said. "How could you let this maniac do this to us?"

"He's the governor, and he might very soon be the president."

"Look I don't know what type of brainwashing you have been subjected to, but no man should submit to slavery to a crazed bigoted lunatic like this guy. As soon as I get out of here I'm going to go back to the police station and you had better believe that I am going to press charges against this person."

George began laughing hysterically. "You really have gone

crazy!"

"I've gone crazy?!"

"You are going to go to the police station as a Negro and expect them to do anything other than perhaps give you a vicious beating and bring you right back here so that master Jefferson can beat you as well?"

"I have been a police officer for over 10 years. I think that when I tell them that some crazy maniac has kidnapped me and forced me into some type of slavery they will be pretty quick to arrest this psycho."

George felt Toby's head. "You got a fever or something? You really think you're a police officer?" George couldn't help but laugh.

"What's so funny?" an African-American woman asked as she came over to them.

"Sally you have to hear this, Toby here thinks that he is a police officer!" George said as both he and Sally began laughing.

"Oh Toby you are a funny one," Sally said as she gave him a playful shove.

"I don't see what's so funny about the situation that we find ourselves in," Toby said. "Aren't any of you bothered by the fact that we have been kidnapped by a crazy person?"

"You're the funny one Toby, a Negro as a police officer. Police officers are there to arrest people like us, to bring us back to our masters when we are disobedient or try to escape. They would never make one of us a police officer."

"Am I the only one here who is not completely insane?" Toby asked as he looked at all of the other men and women in the room staring at him.

"Hey, you niggers get your lazy asses out here," said another white man as he came into the room. "If you want to have your breakfast hurry the hell up as we have a lot of work to do today. When you slack off it reflects badly on me as your overseer, and if any of you thinks that you can get away with goofing off on an important day like today make no mistake that it would give me immense pleasure to give you a whipping later on."

"Who the hell was that son of a bitch?" Toby whispered to George.

"That son of a bitch is McDonald, and he is the one who is going to whip your ass if you decide to be disobedient. And he will probably whip all of our asses as an example as well, so don't let you get us all in trouble. Now come on, let's go eat our breakfast."

Toby could see that whoever these people were, they seemed to have totally developed Stockholm syndrome or something and have given in to their kidnappers, and they seemed to believe whatever garbage that they are feeding them. He figured he had better play it safe until he could think of a plan of escape.

He also realized that in spite of everything he was rather hungry, even though his stomach still felt a little bit troubled after the powerful shock that he had received earlier.

When they went into the mess hall it was just one big table without chairs with a bowl full of bacon in the center of the table.

"Eat up and hurry!" McDonald said.

Toby grabbed a handful of bacon and began chewing on it. "This isn't even warm!"

"You expect them to cook our meals?" George asked as he shoved a bunch of bacon into his mouth. "Just be glad that we are actually getting some meat today."

After eating the cold bacon and washing it down with nothing more than water Toby and all of the other African-American men and women, all wearing collars, were escorted into a room and lined up.

"Now today is a very important day," McDonald said. "Today the governor is receiving delegates from our allies in Germany who want to help his campaign for President. He doesn't want anything to go wrong and wants this house to be a model of obedience, to prove to our Nazi allies that America is not the uncouth land that many still believe it is. We are an advanced industrial nation, built up on the time-honored tradition of slavery. So anyone who thinks that they are going to slack off today, or be disobedient, know that you will pay in blood later. My whip is eager to do some cracking, so I will not hesitate to beat anyone who doesn't keep up the pace and make a good impression on our foreign dignitaries. Now get to work!"

Toby could swear it looked like McDonald put his hand over

his crotch when he mentioned whipping them. He sounded like a real sick sadist and that was all the more reason why Toby had to get his ass out of there as soon as possible. Who knew what these crazy people were going to do next?

Toby and the other slaves quickly got to work cleaning the house to make it spotless. Toby didn't say much more to anyone and figured that he had better keep quiet until he got a better feel for the situation. As he went around cleaning the house he couldn't help but notice that master Jefferson had all sorts of portraits of what looked like Confederate generals, a large bust of Thomas Jefferson and all sorts of Confederate flags and Nazi flags all over the place. This guy was some type of hard-core racist for sure and this just made Toby even more nervous that if he didn't get out of there soon he would probably end up being killed.

Once Toby had finished cleaning the house it was lunchtime and the dignitaries had arrived. Toby opened the door and helped lead the dignitaries in. As he led these men dressed in Nazi uniforms into a house full of Confederate flags, he couldn't help but start to feel sick. How well-connected was this Jefferson guy? Was he the head of the Aryan brotherhood or something?

It was Toby's job to stand there in the dining room as Mr. Jefferson had dinner with a bunch of Nazis.

"As you can see the governor's mansion here is a model of the efficiency of slavery," Mr. Jefferson said. "Every single nigger knows his place and knows the consequences for disobedience. My ancestor and great great great great great grandfather Thomas Jefferson was a slave owner and I come from a long line of slave owning aristocrats. I can trace my lineage back to the founding fathers themselves."

"This is all very impressive," said one of the Nazis as he took a bite of a chicken leg. "But we follow the news in America. You speak about how efficient you have been running your system of slavery, yet all we hear on the news is how every week it seems like your country is suffering another slave uprising, rebellion or some other type of violence. This suggests that you do not have quite as good control of your Negro slaves as you say you do."

"Which is exactly why I am running for president," Mr.

Jefferson said as he took a sip of wine poured by Toby. "President Clifton has always been soft on the Negro question. Oh, he's a white supremacist for sure, but he doesn't realize that you have to take a more hard-liner stance on the slavery question. He doesn't want to damage the property of wealthy slave-owners, so he suggests that we do not use the most violent force necessary to put down the slave uprisings. I say if a slave owner cannot keep his niggers under control then he can't blame the state for killing them in defense of good honest decent white folks. That is why I suggest that slave-owners be charged for the damage that their slaves do. I realize this is not the most popular position to take seeing as it is the campaign funds of the slave owning aristocrats that determine who will win the election, but I am trying to point out to the voters that if we take Pres. Clifton's soft stance on slavery it threatens the stability of the entire institution."

The Nazi put down his chicken leg. "A hard-liner stance is necessary to deal with the mongrel peoples of the world. When the international Zionist conspiracy was threatening to take over the world, we did not hesitate to do what was necessary and wiped them all out. We would razz the ghettos, fill the concentration camps and not hesitate to do what was ever necessary to put down any rebellion. And I think that we have been quite successful in that regard. The Third Reich is the ultimate model of efficiency. Granted America has made many strides in policing and controlling their unruly Negro population, but you have yet to achieve the fine apparatus of a complete and total police state like we have in the Reich. There are very few rebellions because the second there is an uprising it is put down as brutally and efficiently as possible, a total scorched-earth policy."

Mr. Jefferson put down his glass of wine. "I agree, I have read much about the history of the Third Reich and I greatly admire everything that you have managed to do. I want to model the Confederate states on the system that you have set up in Europe and Russia and throughout most of the civilized world. That is why if I am elected president I want to be able to count on the continued support and close supervision of our allies in the Third Reich. We have course appreciate everything that the Reich has done for the

Confederacy so far, but I would like to make our ties stronger. We have similar beliefs and ideals, and I think that if we work together we can legitimately make sure that the white man continues to dominate the earth over the lower peoples of the world."

"You can count on our continued support and we will do everything possible to help you to come into office," the Nazi said as he took a sip of wine. "The third Reich regards the Confederate states as being vital to keeping order and white domination in your hemisphere of the world. We have already helped you to dominate the colored peoples of North and South America and we want to keep that in place. You have heard of the domino effect. If white supremacy fails in North and South America, then it could go on to threaten the stability of white supremacy elsewhere in the world."

"I am very familiar with this theory, which is why I appreciate the continued support that the Third Reich continues to give to the Confederate states. Let us work together to ensure that the future of the world belongs to the white man and not to the racially degenerate races of the world who threaten to pollute mankind with their inferior genetics."

Mr. Jefferson toasted to his Nazi guests and they all took a drink of wine to celebrate.

"Now come gentlemen, let me show you the shooting range that I have put in the back of the governor's mansion," Mr. Jefferson said as he led his guests to the backyard and motioned for Toby to go with them.

Toby stood there and held Mr. Jefferson's ammunition as he and his Nazi companions took turns firing at a target range full of pictures of Abraham Lincoln sitting on a throne with a crown on his head and devil horns.

"Damn nigger lover!" Mr. Jefferson said as he shot a portrait of Abraham Lincoln right between the eyes. "Long live the Confederacy!"

Once they had finished the shooting gallery they were taken on a tour of the governor's mansion and then at the end of the day all of the slaves gathered for a final meal that was also of cold bacon.

"You're quiet tonight Toby," said George. "Is everything okay?"

"Is everything okay?! Is everything okay?! No, it's not okay. Am I the only person who is bothered by the insanity that we are living under?"

"We've never known anything different," George said as he nibbled on his bacon. "You act like suddenly this was something new."

"It is something new! Aren't any of you bothered by the fact that we have been kidnapped by some type of white supremacist who put shock collars on us?"

Everyone stared at Toby like he was a raving lunatic. "I think maybe you should get some rest," George finally said. "You definitely seem to be under the weather. You better not let the master catch you talking like that or you'll get a whipping."

"Oh don't worry, I don't intend to speak any unnecessary words in his presence," Toby said as he finished up his dinner. "I think that I will go to sleep, maybe I will wake up to find that this has all been a bad dream."

As Toby went back to the room where they all slept on uncomfortable cots he found himself unable to sleep as he could hear the sounds of a woman screaming in the other room.

"What's that noise?" Toby asked as he shook George awake.

"What noise?" George asked as he yawned. "I'm trying to get some sleep here."

"What noise?! I am talking about the fact that a few doors down I can hear a woman screaming."

"It's probably just McDonald or master Jefferson having their way with one of the slave women."

"And we're just supposed to sit here like it's not happening?"

"There's nothing we can do about it. That's just the way things are."

Toby shook his head. "I'm a police officer dammit, my job is to serve and protect the public. I can't stand by while a crime is being committed."

"If you interrupt the master he will surely shock you and give you a beating like you can't even imagine. Just let it go Toby."

As much as he wanted to intervene and stop a woman from being raped, there was very little he could do. That was when he was overcome with a feeling of profound helplessness. Here he was locked in the room with a shock collar around him completely unable to stop the crime that was going on just a few doors down.

Toby tried to sleep amidst the sound of screams, but he felt that he would not be able to sleep tonight. As soon as he saw the opportunity he had every intention of getting out of here as soon as possible. If he was a slave, it was time to start a slave revolt.

He just didn't know how on earth he would do it.

Chapter 5

Roy woke up the next morning in bed with Charlotte and he was glad that it was finally his day off as he didn't feel like he could take another day of going to work after what he had witnessed just the other day.

"Did you sleep well last night darling," Charlotte said as she kissed him.

"I've slept better before," Roy said as he got up and got dressed.

"Why are you getting dressed so soon," Charlotte said as she made amorous glances at him. "It's Saturday and I know that you like to stay in bed on Saturday. There have been so many riots lately that you have hardly gotten any days off."

"Well hey, what can you do?"

Charlotte stretched her arms and yawned. "I know, the nigger problem is becoming worse every single day. Why can't the slaves just learn to be obedient and obey their masters? Do they really have it so bad? I mean we provide them with food and shelter and everything that simple creatures like them could possibly want. Honestly it's getting so terrible that it's frightening to go outside now. I know the police officers like you are doing a good job but every time I leave the house I still worry that I'm going to be raped or assaulted by some type of savage African hoodlum."

"Look I am sure that things will get better and they will calm down in a short amount of time. We have the best police department around and we will contain the problem."

"Oh I have no doubt that you will dear. And you know how it just gets me so hot and bothered thinking of you out there shooting all of those degenerate Negroes."

"Hey do you think maybe we could talk about something else?"

"Of course, you have to deal with niggers all week long that you probably don't want to hear about it on your one day off, your one day when you can bask in the happy glow of being with your all-white family without having to see a single black face to offend the eye."

"Thank you, I appreciate it."

"There is just one question that I have wondered though on the topic of slaves and slavery."

"What is that?"

"A lot of people always ask me, seeing as you are the top slave catcher around here, why don't we have any slaves ourselves? You know that with every slave that we get that's more voting power we have and it is an election year, when there are often sales on slaves. We could probably get one really cheap."

"Aren't you afraid that they're going to rape you or cut your throat in the middle of the night?"

"I'm afraid of the ones out there on the street but if we get one that is well-trained at one of the top slave training academies, one that's nice and docile, I mean I think that that would be good to help around the house. I don't think that we should get a male slave of course, we should get a female slave, one that's easier to control."

"But wouldn't that make you jealous," Roy said jokingly before he realized he probably shouldn't have mentioned anything like that.

"Why would I be jealous? I know that you're not one of those men who gets all crazy for nigger women. I know that you're a good upstanding Christian who would never commit some act of bestiality like that. I know that there are a lot of men who are like that and that you probably know quite a few of them, but I know that you think it's downright indecent, having sex with people of a different race like that. I mean these people are basically animals."

"Of course they are," Roy said now feeling again uncomfortable with the whole situation.

"I'm sorry if I made you uncomfortable dear. I know that in

your profession you kind of have to be around niggers all day and the idea of having one in our home might be unsettling since you know how violent these people can be. And I know that you are worried that some of them might be acting as spies or part of the slave resistance like so many are these days, but I really think that it might be a good investment to perhaps look into getting maybe a really young docile female slave, or perhaps an elderly one. An elderly slave shouldn't be that much trouble and they go very cheap since they can only do a limited amount of work. I know that we have that Mexican women, what was her name, Consuela, that we have to watch the children occasionally, but it's not the same as having the 24 hour supervision of a regular nanny. And it would be nice to have some help around the house while you're away all day."

"I'll think about it," Roy said knowing that he certainly was not going to think about it because he had already thought about it more than he ever wanted to. The idea that he was discussing purchasing a slave with his wife was making him feel even sicker than he had been the night before.

"I'll go make breakfast," Charlotte said as she got dressed and went into the kitchen. She began cooking bacon and eggs as she seemed to be humming some type of tune that Roy did not recognize.

"How are you today kids," Roy said as his kids ran up to him and started grabbing him by the leg.

"We love you dad," Bonnie said.

"Did mom ask you about getting a slave," Atticus said.

"Atticus!" Charlotte shouted. "I'm sorry dear; I know you don't want to talk about the slavery issue at the breakfast table. Now Atticus I have discussed the slave matter with your father and he will think about it."

"We should really get a slave dad," Atticus said. "Slaves are cool because they have to do whatever you want and they can't say no. My friend Billy Baxter, his family has five slaves, can you imagine that, five whole slaves!"

"We're not made of money," Roy said even though looking at his house he realized that he was of considerably better economic means than he had been before and probably could easily afford at least one or two slaves if he so desired, but of course he didn't. "Now let's sit down and eat our breakfast like a family."

"Let's watch our favorite TV show," Atticus said as he turned on the television.

"And what exactly is our favorite TV show?" Roy asked as he rolled his eyes afraid of what the answer might be.

"National nigger fights!" Atticus and Bonnie both shouted as they squealed with glee and flipped on the TV to what looked like a bunch of shirtless black men in some type of an arena beating the living hell out of each other.

"I hope this is just another form of boxing," Roy said, but he didn't see any boxing gloves anywhere to be seen.

"Boxing is boring!" Atticus said.

"Yeah, boring!" Bonnie said as she stuck out her tongue.

"National nigger fights is the greatest show in the world," Atticus said as he stared at the screen. "You take some slaves and they just start beating the hell out of each other and people bet on it and sometimes they even end up fighting right to the death."

"But that's just barbaric!" Roy shouted.

"Sometimes the slaves win their freedom and sometimes freemen even volunteer to fight for the money," Bonnie said. "But that's kind of ridiculous."

"What is kind of ridiculous?" Roy asked.

"A free black man, black people are supposed to be our servants, we can't have them running around freely," Bonnie said. "That would just mean more trouble for you wouldn't it daddy?"

Roy couldn't help but notice that Bonnie and Charlotte both seemed to be staring at the chests of the black men with rather wide eyes. Considering that Bonnie was just a little girl that was especially disturbing.

"I don't think that you kids should be watching something this violent," Roy said. "I see violence like this all the time and it's not something that we should be celebrating, it's not pretty."

Roy changed the channel to what looked like the shopping network.

"Today on the home shopping channel we have some great slaves that are going for value prices," the auctioneer said as they pointed to a black man standing on a pedestal. "As you can see the slaves have been certified by a doctor to be fully healthy and have many years of good work ahead of them. These slaves are well trained to respond obediently to their master's every whim and there is a money back guarantee that if the slaves have not been properly conditioned that they can be sent back for reconditioning until they are obedient and docile."

"Let's just watch the news," Roy said as he went to the news channel.

"I vow that if I am elected to be your president that I will crack down hard on all these disobedient slaves," said Thomas Jefferson, the governor who was running for president against president Clifton. "Our nation can be great once again. When my ancestors founded this country under the great institution of slavery the slaves knew their place. Now in the modern age slaves have begun getting more uppity, have been resisting our great institutions and challenging our institutions that were ordained by God himself. If I am elected I guarantee that there will be a crackdown. Every slave will be more carefully monitored and we will have chips implanted in all of them, it will be mandatory and not voluntary anymore. We will give the police greater authority to put down these rebellions, to arrest degenerate subversives like abolitionists. President Clifton has been too easy on the abolitionists and I suspect that he has abolitionist sympathies. If you want a country that will be great again, a country that will be obedient again, vote for Thomas Jefferson."

"His name is actually Thomas Jefferson," Roy said shaking his head. "Just like our original founding father."

Charlotte smiled and nodded. "He is a descendent of Thomas Jefferson, so you know that he has greatness in his blood. There are some who say that President Clifton might not be as racially pure as he says he is. Thomas Jefferson can assert that he has one of the most racially pure lines of any President we have had since the founding of the Confederate states."

"Greatness isn't a matter of what blood you have, it comes from your character," Roy said shaking his head.

Charlotte nodded. "Of course character is important, but we

know that people who aren't racially pure often have shady characters. Remember back when we had president Oxford a while back? He was a rampant womanizer, an alcoholic and sympathetic towards Jews. And lo and behold research into his ancestry found that at one point he even had black and Jewish ancestors down the line. No wonder he was such a terrible President. Honestly I wish they would have passed that resolution making every member of the government undergo a rigorous blood test to make sure that they are fully racially pure, to make sure there is nothing wrong with them. You know that that is the case with our allies in Germany. Everyone there has to pass a racial purity test to hold even the smallest government office and I think that we should follow their lead. We can't expect our country to be great if our country isn't pure. Members of the Nazi party have to be able to trace their ancestry back a few generations to prove that there aren't any Jews or other degenerate races in their ancestry, and that is definitely the right thing to do and we should emulate them."

"Look the Nazis are great and everything," Roy said trying to hold his tongue and not gag at that statement. "But sometimes I think that maybe this country is emulating them a little bit too much. I think that we have to be our own nation as well, you know what I mean?"

"Of course I do dear," Charlotte said as she ate some of her bacon." It's just that the Nazis are our closest allies and they're helping us to protect white supremacy in this area of the globe. You know about the domino theory of course. If the white race falls here in America it might start falling elsewhere in the world, so they are well motivated to keep us in power here. At your job aren't they trying to model the police model on the Gestapo in Nazi Germany? There's no greater police force in the entire world than what they have in Nazi Germany. That's what we should aspire to be like, we should be aspiring to be as great as Germany."

"It's my day off I would rather not discuss politics," Roy said as he started stuffing his face full of bacon so he would have an excuse not to talk.

"I was hoping that today maybe you could spend some time with the children," Charlotte said.

"I'd love to spend time with the children," Roy said as he continued eating his bacon. "What would you kids like to do today? Maybe we could do something nice and quiet like play a board game."

"Can we play nigger hunt?" Bonnie said causing Roy to begin choking on his bacon.

"Are you okay dear?" Charlotte said as Roy continued choking on his bacon before spitting it up in the sink.

"I'm fine," Roy said. He was most certainly not fine. He seemed like he couldn't go more than five minutes without someone bringing up something about niggers or slaves or the racial question. He was starting to understand what Toby must have felt. Race had ever been such a big part of his life but now that he was seeing racism raw and uncensored from his own family it was starting to make him really sick.

"I love nigger hunt except I always lose," Atticus said shaking his head. "Besides the videogame version is better."

"There's a videogame version?" Roy asked.

"Yeah, it's the greatest videogame in the world, you get to go around hunting slaves and shooting them," Atticus said. "Last week I managed to beat my high score. I managed to shoot over 63 niggers."

"You know son shooting niggers isn't always a great thing," Roy said.

"I know I know, like you always told me, you should never shoot niggers because they might be someone's property," Atticus said. "But it's okay, it's just a videogame."

"But sometimes videogames don't always teach you the best of things."

"You're not going to use that tired old argument that videogames make people violent and crazy," Atticus said as he shook his head.

Roy went over to the videogame console and picked up some of the games that the children had. One of them seemed like you got to run a concentration camp, one you got to be a Gestapo officer in Nazi Germany and it seemed like half of his videogames involved the Civil War or Nazi Germany in some way, with the Confederacy and the Nazis being the good guys of course.

"Maybe it would be best if you kids spend some time playing outside," Roy said.

"Is it really safe for the children to go outside, what with all the racial violence and everything," Charlotte said.

"I just mean in the backyard where things will be nice and safe and we can keep an eye on the children," Roy said.

"Maybe you can teach me how to shoot a gun," Atticus said with a big smile.

"You're 12 years old!" Roy shouted.

"I know, I'm 12 years old and I still haven't learned how to shoot a gun, but what if some type of crazy nigger started trying to kill me or trying to rape Bonnie or mom? Besides I want to grow up to be a slave catcher just like you dad, hunting down violent niggers and shooting them. I want to be a hero and serve my country."

Roy looked into Atticus's eyes and he saw a gleam that he didn't really feel comfortable with so he simply put his hand on Atticus's shoulder and patted it. "Son there are a lot of ways to be a hero and to serve your country, it's not all about slave catching and shooting people. Do you understand?"

Atticus shrugged his shoulders. "I guess so."

"Now come on son, let's go play outside," Roy said as his children followed him outside.

Over the next couple of hours the children played in the backyard and went swimming in the pool but soon it was starting to get dark out. Roy had to admit that as he watched his children playing in the pool and just relaxed he was starting to feel better, like nothing else could possibly go wrong.

That was when he heard a scream.

"Bonnie!" Roy shouted and that was when he looked up to see a black man holding a knife up to Bonnie's throat.

"Look mister I don't want to hurt her but I will," the man said as he put the knife up to her throat. "I just want to escape up north; I promise that I will leave your family alone if you just help me to get up north."

"Look just put the knife down, I am a police officer," Roy said as he tried to de-escalate the situation.

"You're a slave catcher," the man said as he continued to hold the knife up to Bonnie's throat as she stood there trembling and apparently was also wetting her pants.

"Daddy help me," Bonnie said as tears streamed down her cheeks.

Roy was unarmed and he wasn't exactly sure what he should do in this situation. He had been trained to calm people down in these type of situations but the slave looked positively deranged. As Roy stared into the eyes of this man holding a knife to his daughter's throat suddenly he felt something rage up inside of him. Suddenly all of his feelings about racism and the injustice of slavery faded away and he just saw a violent maniac trying to harm his family.

Roy put up his hand and slowly walked towards the man and that was when he heard a gunshot fire as the man dropped his knife, grabbed his chest and fell over.

"Daddy!" Bonnie said as she ran into her father's arms and began crying.

"It's okay sweetie, it's okay, Daddy's here," Roy said as he hugged a still trembling Bonnie. But that was when he had another thought but before he could even process that thought he got his answer to his question of who shot the slave.

"That's how you deal with niggers," Atticus said as he came up from behind the body of the dead man and stood there holding Roy's handgun and smiling.

If Roy wasn't already sick before, and he was, he knew that now his bacon would be coming up in short order and there was nothing in the world that could prevent that.

Chapter 6

Toby found it difficult to sleep that night knowing what was going on just a few doors down. Being a police officer and being unable to stop an innocent woman from being raped was perhaps the most terrible thing that he had ever experienced.

The next morning as the slaves were woken up bright and early Toby couldn't help but notice Sally was walking with a limp.

"Sally," Toby said. "Are you okay?"

"I'm fine," Sally said with a look of pain on her face.

"But you are most certainly not fine. I heard what Mr. Jefferson was doing to you last night. How could you let him do that to you?" Toby immediately felt bad as soon as he said that. He didn't want to blame the victim but the fact that she was able to do nothing to stop Mr. Jefferson from raping her was making his blood boil.

"I don't know what you are talking about Toby, but I have to start preparing the breakfast for master as I would not want to displease him by not having breakfast on the table when he wakes up."

"He raped you last night!"

Sally gave Toby a look of astonishment.

"Why are you looking at me like that?" Toby asked.

"A white man can't rape a colored woman," Sally said shaking her head.

"What the hell are you talking about? Rape is rape; color has nothing to do with it!"

"What the hell are you talking about? Of course color has everything to do with it. I am master Jefferson's property, he can do whatever he wants with me. It's only rape when a colored person rapes a white woman."

"Don't tell me you actually believe that!"

"Of course I believe that, that's the way things are, that's the law. If a colored person rapes a white person they'll be executed, but if a white person wants to have their way with a colored person you just have to submit, there's nothing you can do."

"This isn't right!"

"I don't want to talk about it," Sally said as she pushed Toby away.

Toby didn't want to press the issue but it was infuriating him that Sally could accept something so horrible as though it were normal.

"Is something the matter here Toby," McDonald said as he came down the hall. "Don't you have lots of important work to do, the both of you?"

"I'm sorry Mr. McDonald, I will be getting to my work shortly," Sally said. "I was just having a brief conversation with Toby who doesn't realize that we are supposed to be working right now."

Sally started limping off clearly in a lot of pain from what had happened last night but held her head high as though it didn't bother her.

"Causing trouble again I see Toby," McDonald said as he grabbed Toby by the cheeks and looked at him.

"Get your hands off of me," Toby said as he smacked away McDonald's hand.

"You dare raise your hand to me boy!" McDonald said as he pressed a button on his remote causing a powerful shock to go through Toby's body causing him to fall to the floor and begin convulsing for a moment before the effect wore off. McDonald then kicked him in the stomach. "You had better learn your place around here boy or I will give you a more powerful shock next time. Consider that a warning. If you continue to be disobedient like this you won't just get a shock but you will get a whipping as well and we will make an example of you. Now everything has to go perfectly as master Jefferson is having lots of important guests again. This is an election season and we have to put up the front that this is a happy home full of happy obedience slaves, you get what I am saying boy?"

Toby was absolutely fuming but he knew if he mouthed off to this man again it might end up costing him his life.

"Yes," Toby said as McDonald put his foot down on Toby's neck.

"I don't know if I heard you properly boy," McDonald said. "What did you say?"

"Yes master McDonald," Toby said as McDonald gradually moved his foot off of Toby's throat.

"That's better," McDonald said as he shook his head. "There's nothing I hate more in this world than an uppity arrogant nigger who doesn't know his place. Well you had better learn your place quickly boy or you are going to be in a world of pain. You should feel privileged to be the personal slave of a man as prestigious as Mr. Jefferson. If things go according to plan soon he will be the next president of the Confederate states of America. Now I want you to make yourself presentable and get your ass to work."

Toby went to the breakfast hall where he once again had his monotonous diet of cold bacon but he couldn't help but spend the entire time watching Sally. He could see the look of sadness in Sally's eyes as she was slowly nibbling on her bacon and he could see that every couple of minutes she stopped to hold her stomach.

He barely had an appetite because as he watched Sally suffering from the pains of her abuse he was beginning to feel sick to his stomach. Violence and abuse of women like that was something that he could not tolerate under any circumstances. He had witnessed too much of it in his own life and every time he saw that it made his blood run cold and he just wanted to murder the perpetrator himself. He had never in the line of duty had to kill another individual, for which he was thankful, but when he met with people who were guilty of domestic abuse he was tempted to take them out back and give them a taste of their own medicine. It was always hard for him to control himself under those circumstances but now he needed his police training more than ever.

"Okay niggers, chow time is over, now clean up after yourselves you dirty animals," McDonald said. "This place has to be absolutely spotless as we are having reporters coming to do a personal interview of the great master Jefferson, and you are all to be on your best behavior or I have orders to beat the living hell out of you. If you think that I have beaten the hell out of you before you haven't seen anything yet. We are going to present this place as a model of decorum and the efficiency of the system of slavery. One little slip up and you will be paying for it, believe me."

Toby began cleaning up the kitchen but as he was doing so he couldn't help but keep looking over at Sally who was clearly in a lot of pain and struggling to do her daily tasks.

"Eyes on your work nigger," McDonald said as he smacked Toby in the side with a rubber truncheon. "You nigger men, you really are animals. All you think about is screwing and fucking everything that lives and breathes."

That wasn't me, that was actually the master, Toby wanted to shout out, but he held his tongue because he knew if he didn't he would be getting more than a rubber truncheon to the side. He had to find some way to get out of there and to help Sally escape but right now he didn't have the slightest clue on how to do that.

"Well you can take care of your Dick later on your own time," McDonald said as he smacked Toby again with a rubber truncheon. "God you creatures breed like animals. Soon you're going to out breed the white race, it's even become a major election issue, you people are growing too numerous. We should make it mandatory neutering after a couple of children have been sired or after a certain age, but of course slave owners wouldn't like that because they always need to create new slaves to replace the old and dying ones or to sell off."

Toby really never like discussing politics but now in this new world that he found himself in he really hated hearing anything political. He knew that the world he came from was racist but this was racism on steroids and it was almost universally accepted as normal.

After the slaves finished cleaning up after breakfast they were all ordered onto the lawn to stand at attention behind master Jefferson as he talked to a bunch of reporters.

"As you can see I take the best of care of my slaves," master Jefferson said as he lifted up the lips of one slave and pointed to his white teeth. "As you can see the slaves have dental care and great health care. In fact they have healthcare that would be the envy of a lot of white men. I think that a lot of the slaves don't realize how well that they have it, as taking care of all their needs such as food, shelter and medical concerns. Maintaining slaves can be extremely expensive and I think that a lot of people don't realize just how well taken care of these slaves are."

"But are they happy?" the reporter said as he held up a microphone. Toby couldn't help but notice that all of the reporters were white men and the women were just in the background completely silent.

"Well why don't we ask them ourselves," Mr. Jefferson said as he looked over at Toby. "This is my long-term slave Toby; he's one of my house niggers. Do I not take good care of you Toby?"

Toby wanted to shout that he was a disgusting vile rapist since they were being televised at that exact moment but he knew that if he said that it would be the end of his life right then and there.

"Yes master, you take excellent care of all of us, we all are lucky to be serving under you," Toby said. "We can only hope and pray that you win this election so that you can continue making this country great again."

"Well spoken, especially for a slave," the reporter said. "There is a controversial measure that many people think should be passing through the Senate suggesting that maybe slaves should be educated, what do you think about that Mr. Jefferson?"

Mr. Jefferson laughed. "Education for niggers, I can't think of a more useless waste of taxpayer money. What do niggers need to be educated for? An educated nigger is a dangerous nigger. You start educating niggers and they start getting ideas in their heads, which is the last thing that you want. Education for niggers is just a load of abolitionist propaganda because these people want to destabilize our perfect institution of slavery that has been in place for hundreds of years. They hate tradition, they hate this country, and they hate the white race, which is why we are having so many riots lately. Look at this slave," Mr. Jefferson said as he tapped his fingers on Toby's head. "Do you think that there is anything inside of there? Of course not. An empty headed nigger is a happy nigger, isn't that right Toby?"

"Yes master, no thoughts in this head of mine," Toby said as he started doing a little dance that made him look like an imbecile as several people in the audience began laughing and clapping.

"You see these people are happy to laugh and dance and sing and to serve their superior white masters," Mr. Jefferson said. "Even the Bible said that the curse of ham is upon them and that they were meant to be simple people and to serve others. God himself has ordained this destiny for niggers and I last thing I'm about to do is go against the will of Almighty God."

"What about you miss, are you happy?" a reporter said as he put his microphone up to Sally's face.

Toby found his teeth grinding and he was trying his best to control himself. But as he saw Sally standing there still looking in pain he saw her lift up her head and force a smile.

"I'm very happy," Sally said. "Master Jefferson is the best master in the entire world and I couldn't picture any master who didn't care more for his slaves and his niggers than he does. We can only hope to God that soon he will be the next president and restore traditional values like the infallible institution of slavery."

People began clapping as Toby could see Sally looking down at her feet in a submissive posture. He could tell just by looking at her that she was trying not to cringe in the presence of master Jefferson. In fact just looking at him was probably causing her to remember all the things that he did to her just last night, and no doubt probably hundreds or thousands of times before.

"Mr. Jefferson what are you going to do about the so-called epidemic of nigger rape," the reporter asked. "It has become a heated issue in the election that with all of these slave uprisings it's not even safe for women to go out anymore. Some people say that a curfew for slaves isn't enough because it's getting difficult to enforce. The number of people who have been raped has skyrocketed recently. If you were elected as president what would you do to combat this dramatic rise in sexual assault at the hands of violent African savages?"

"Well I'm glad that you asked that question," Mr. Jefferson said with a big smile. "There's nothing in this world that I find more disgusting than a vile degenerate rapist, a creature that is completely driven by impulse and unable to control even their most basic urges. Of course we all know that niggers are barely above the animal level so that we have to treat them like animals sometimes. That is why I advocate that any niggers that are caught raping a white woman suffer mandatory castration or possibly even death. I favor the death penalty for rapists. If there is any greater goal as President of these great Confederate states it is to protect the virtue of white womanhood from these vile nigger scum."

That response was met with thunderous applause from everyone in the audience. It took every bit of restraint that Toby had in his body to avoid shouting out and screaming at Mr. Jefferson. He was grinding his teeth so hard that it was beginning to hurt.

"Thank you for asking all these questions Mr. future President," the reporter said as Mr. Jefferson laughed and smiled and shook his hand.

"Don't forget a vote for Jefferson is a vote for a safe America, a better America, a greater America."

People continued cheering and taking all sorts of pictures as the rest of the slaves were led back to their quarters for the rest of the day so that they would be out of sight of all the reporters.

As Toby went back to his quarters for the day he couldn't help but see that Sally was in the corner crying. He wanted to go over and comfort her but that was when McDonald came and started leading her away.

"Where are you taking her?" Toby asked as he approached McDonald.

"Well that is none of your business boy," McDonald said as he raised his remote in Toby's general direction.
"Now you better back off or you're going to be on the floor shitting those pantaloons of yours that the master was so generous enough to provide for you."

Toby wanted to follow but as he stood there feeling the collar around his neck that could shock him to death at the press of a button, he once again realized that he was totally helpless to do anything and once again he had never been angrier.

But he held his tongue, although he knew that he couldn't hold it for much longer. He was going to have to do something and he was going to have to do something soon.

<u>Chapter 7</u>

Roy couldn't stop vomiting as Charlotte just began crying and hugging Atticus and Bonnie.

"Oh my little babies," Charlotte said as she sobbed hysterically. "Are you okay?"

"I think so but I wet myself," Bonnie said as she continued crying.

"It's okay darling we can wash those or we get you new clothes, the important thing is that you are safe thanks to your heroic brother," Charlotte said as she kissed Atticus on the head.

"Aw mom it was nothing," Atticus said clearly embarrassed by the way his mom was treating him.

"It was not nothing," Roy said as he turned to Atticus. "You killed a man today son. You are only 12 years old and you killed a man."

"I just killed a nigger, a slave," Atticus said. "If I didn't he would probably have raped or killed Bonnie and mom, that's the way you have to deal with niggers, you know that father, you deal with these people all day every day."

"Atticus you don't just go around killing people," Roy said as he continued to feel sick. "I don't care if they are black or white, slave or free."

"I know I shouldn't shoot a slave because it someone's property but I was just defending myself," Atticus said. "It's the right of every single citizen, nay the obligation of every single citizen, to protect themselves and to protect others around them. That's what they always teach in the junior patriot league. I don't see why you are getting so crazy dad; you kill people all the time."

"I don't kill people unless I absolutely have to."

"Don't be hard on him, he's a hero, he saved his sister," Charlotte said as Bonnie ran over and hugged Atticus.

It didn't take more than a minute or two before they heard the sounds of police sirens approaching the house.

"I had better go take care of this," Roy said as he opened the door and let the police officers in and guided them around to the back where the body of the slave was still lying in a pool of blood.

"Was anybody hurt?" officer Grady said as he arrived on the scene.

"No fortunately not," Roy said. "The slave tried to attack my daughter with a knife but my son shot him."

"That's a good boy you've got there," officer Grady said as he patted Roy on the shoulder. "You taught him very well and you should be proud of him. There are not many 12-year-old boys I know who can keep their cool and stand up when they are being attacked by a dangerous savage nigger like that. He will probably make a good police officer one day, maybe he will even become a slave catcher like you are. We're just lucky that the slave was stupid enough to jump over the fence into the yard of a police officer, a slave catcher on top of that. But these people aren't very bright; if they were they wouldn't be trying to escape all the time. They would realize how good they have it under slavery and they would accept it as the natural order."

"Where did this slave escape from?" Roy asked.

"He escaped from a plantation not too far from here, apparently murdered his master in cold blood and then made a run for it. We are just glad that your son managed to stop him before any of your family was hurt. It really is getting ridiculous; even in a nice white neighborhood like this you can't be free from attacks by violent savage niggers."

"But would you believe this is the first day I have had off in quite a while too."

"God it's sad," officer Grady said as he shook his head. "You can't even enjoy a weekend with your family without having to deal with violent crazy niggers like this. Let's just hope that Thomas Jefferson is the next president because he will crack down on these maniacs in a way that a nigger loving abolitionist sympathizing bastard like President Clifton would never even dream of."

As they were talking workers came and started photographing the crime scene and slowly removing the body of the dead black man in their backyard.

"What was the name?" Roy asked. "The slave, the slave that my son killed, what was his name?"

"His name was Rufus," officer Grady said shaking his head. "Why, does it matter?"

"Yes, yes it matters because I want to know the name of the man my son killed, because I don't want him to forget it."

Officer Grady laughed. "Well of course, every young boy wants to know the name of the first nigger he killed. You really should be proud of that boy of yours, my son's a little pansy who probably would have wet his own pants if he ever saw a black man in the backyard like that, knife or no knife."

"That's not why I wanted to know his name," Roy said still feeling sick to his stomach and now even a little bit lightheaded.

"Hey maybe someday your boy will get it tattooed on his body, not many boys can say that they killed a nigger when they were only 12 years old."

"Look officer Grady I realize that there are procedures that have to be put into place here but I would rather get this over with as soon as possible, as I think that my family has had a very long day and they are very frightened."

"But of course, I fully understand, I know that if some type of savage nigger came into my backyard my little lady probably wouldn't be unable to sleep for a month. Luckily we have a first-class security system; you really can't be too safe now with all these nigger riots and the epidemic of nigger rape going on. My wife is patently terrified to go outside alone, as well she should be. The fairer sex should really stick to what they know best, women belong in the kitchen and the bedroom, not out on the streets, am I right?"

"Yes, sure, whatever," Roy said wanting to end this line of conversation as quickly as possible. "Now if you don't mind I think that I have a lot to talk to my family about."

Once they had cleared the body of Rufus out of the backyard and logged the incident eventually they cleared out and Roy was able to go back to his family.

"What do you want to get for dinner tonight?" Charlotte asked. "After everything that happened I don't even really feel like I have much of an appetite. My pulse is still racing and my heart is still pounding. It used to be this was a safe country where we didn't have to worry about constant nigger rebellions and constant attacks like this. This nation really is going to hell in a hand basket with all these unruly niggers."

"Can we talk about something other than niggers for a change," Roy said. "Is everyone okay, that's the important thing?"

"I'm scared dad, what if another black man comes and attacks us," Bonnie said as her eyes began filling with tears again. "I don't want to be raped, if I'm raped no white man will ever want to marry me."

"Darling you're never going to be raped, I would never let that happen," Roy said.

"I just hate these niggers so much," Bonnie said as she continued crying. "Sometimes I just wish God would kill all of them."

"Bonnie you shouldn't talk like that," Roy said. "Niggers are people too; they are just different than us, that's all."

Charlotte snorted. "Different, they are as different from us as we are from animals. They have more in common with some type of savage wolf than they do with a human being. I wouldn't even really call them people, they are more like animals. They should probably be kept in cages most of the time."

"This is exactly why we shouldn't get a slave," Roy said, taking the opportunity to at least resolve that issue. "I think that under the current conditions that getting a slave would be out of the question, do you agree?" The family all nodded in agreement. "Good, I'm glad that that is resolved at least."

"Instead of getting a slave we should probably get a security system," Charlotte said. "I don't know how you can be the slave catcher general like that and not even have a security system when they are niggers running around rampant. We have to think of the family's safety."

"Well I will certainly think about it," Roy said shaking his head, and in this case he really was thinking about it. He felt ashamed to admit it but after the incident today he had to admit that he was once again finding himself afraid of black people. He had never considered himself a bigot before but right now he just felt total rage. "You know the safety of this family is the most important thing in the world to me and I wouldn't have become a police officer and a slave catcher if I didn't believe that is the God honest truth. Now what does everyone want for dinner?"

They ended up just getting takeout and they ate mostly in silence. They had a lot left over at the end of the night because nobody seemed to be very hungry and nobody felt like cooking or eating, and they decided to go to bed early that night.

Roy went into Atticus's bedroom because he felt like he had to say something more to him, although what exactly he would say in a situation like this he wasn't exactly sure. He wasn't prepared for discussing his child shooting a man.

"Atticus are you awake?" Roy said as he sat down on Atticus's bed which was covered in Confederate flag sheets.

"Yeah dad," Atticus said as he yawned. "I'm kind of tired though."

"Well we all had a very exhausting day, and a very traumatizing day. I just wanted to make sure that you are okay before I go to sleep."

"I'm fine dad, I'm a hero, and I saved the day."

"I am glad that you were able to protect your mother and sister but what you did today was very dangerous. You could have been seriously hurt or your sister could have been seriously hurt if things had gone differently. I also want to realize that killing doesn't make a person a hero. I am proud of you for defending the family but at the same time you have to realize that killing is wrong."

"I realize that killing is wrong dad, but this is self-defense, and it was just a nigger, it wasn't like it was like a real white human being with a soul or anything."

"You don't believe that niggers have souls?"

"Of course not, they are animals, they are subhuman. Only white people have souls because black people cannot be moral and cannot comprehend morality or the Bible."

"Where did you learn that type of thing?"

"Well in church of course dad, in Sunday school. We were taught how God separated all the races, putting the white race at the top to be the guardians of morality. The black races are simple primitive folks, like animals who have been cursed by God, and that is why we are doing the moral duty by trying to civilize the savages and giving them a good home under slavery."

"Well son it's not true that black people can't be moral."

"How could niggers be moral though? They can't even read, which means they can't read the Bible."

"Not all black people are illiterate son."

"But they should be, you know it's illegal to teach slaves to read. I remember when you found that nigger who had an entire library of all sorts of abolitionist literature and was actually trying to publish books. Can you even imagine that, you laughed so hard at the idea of a nigger trying to read and write and actually produce literature. But you taught me that they have no culture and that any attempts for them to read is just sort of mimicry."

"You know son sometimes I don't like to admit this but occasionally your father can be wrong. I think that tomorrow at church I'm going to have to have a word with your Sunday school teacher."

Roy had a restless sleep that night. He could see that Charlotte was also restless and frightened because she stayed close to him and didn't let go of him. However he found himself getting up every hour or so to go look out the window to make sure that nobody was invading his home. He would also go and check on the children because the whole incident had him shaken up.

Every time Roy closed his eyes he just saw Rufus falling down dead and then Atticus standing there holding his gun.

In the middle of the night he went down into his backyard and looked up at the moon and shook his head. "What the hell has happened to me?" Roy said as he looked up to the sky. "Whose life have I walked into?"

Roy realized that he hadn't really asked himself that question very deeply. The world he found himself in was shocking but he never thought to himself just precisely how he became someone else. The man that he had walked into, whose life he now inhabited was not the man that he was yesterday, and it sounds like he was not a person that he would have had a very high opinion of.

Roy got down on his knees and folded his hands in prayer. "God I don't know if you are up there, but if you are please forgive me for anything that I have done and please watch over my family. And wherever Toby might have gone, please watch over him as well. Amen."

But he thought that perhaps this was a punishment from God or some type of message from God. Maybe he had been brought to this new world to confront his own latent bigotry. He had never seen himself as a bigot but now that he found him in this new position in this new society he was starting to realize a lot of things about himself that he wouldn't necessarily have noticed otherwise, and that he also didn't really like.

He resolved that the next morning he would go to church and he would have a discussion with his children's Sunday school teacher.

"Everybody up for church," Charlotte said as she got everyone ready.

As they drove to church they did put on the car radio.

"And in the national news nigger riots continue around the country, with slave uprisings at an all-time high and presidential candidate Thomas Jefferson swearing that if elected he will bring down the hammer of God on these degenerate savages," the radio said before Roy turned it off.

"I just want to go one day without thinking about the problems of the country," Roy said shaking his head.

"Well we know what all the problems of the country are about, it just comes down to niggers this and niggers that," Charlotte said. "All the violence and destruction and instability in this country is caused by niggers."

"Let's not talk about this right now," Roy said. "This is the Lord's day so let's show it the proper respect. I'd rather not listen to all this stuff on the radio while I am driving. If you want to listen to the radio then why don't you drive?"

Charlotte burst out laughing.

"What's so funny?" Roy asked.

"Oh sorry I thought you were making a joke, you said maybe I should drive, a woman driver, that is such a funny joke. Next you're going to ask me whether I want to vote."

Bonnie and Atticus began laughing as well until they were practically in hysterics. Roy didn't exactly find it funny but he decided to laugh along with them so as not to seem out of place, as if he could possibly feel any more out of place.

It didn't take long for them to arrive at church and while the children went off to Sunday school Roy and Charlotte sat up in the front pews to listen to the sermon.

"Children of Christ," the pastor said as he stood up in front of everyone with a big smile on his face. He looked like a really nice friendly sort and it put Roy at ease, for about five seconds until he started talking again.

"Brothers and sisters in the Army of Christ," he began saying as his expression changed. "We are witnessing the beginning of the apocalypse. As foretold in the book of Revelation the forces of Satan are gathering in the form of nigger riots throughout the country. All of our institutions are collapsing, from slavery to religion. People are starting to lose their faith as members of the lower races ravage the land. I have told you this would happen when the end of days was coming. For years I have been warning that someday the slaves were going to rise up and start killing all good Christian white people. That is why I advise you all to bring your guns to church because even here in the Lord's house we are not safe from the forces of Satan, from the sex crazed psychosis of the black man who lives only to menace white people and to defile white women."

Roy looked to his side and saw Charlotte nodding and smiling.

"Isn't he such an eloquent speaker?" Charlotte said with a huge smile.

"But worry not children, for the day of judgment is upon us and soon God is going to cleanse the world of the lower races and make the world safe for his chosen people, the white people, the master race," the pastor said as everyone started shouting and cheering Amen.

"Is this guy for real?" Roy asked.

"He's amazing isn't he?" Charlotte said as she took a fan and began waving in front of her. "I know it may be indecent to say but if I hadn't married you first I wouldn't mind being married to someone like him."

The thought of that made Roy sick to his stomach yet again, as the pastor went on and on in a long protracted sermon where he talked about how the day of judgment was coming, soon there was going to be a race war and that every single white person had to arm themselves and get right with God before the final apocalyptic battle came that would result in the complete destruction of the black race, and the exaltation of God's chosen people to rule over the world forever in perfect whiteness and purity.

"And I would just like to close by saying make sure that you vote for Thomas Jefferson as God has already chosen him," the pastor said.

"Is this a church sermon or a political rally?" Roy said shaking his head.

"If you're not right with God you are not going to be right in your politics either," Charlotte said. "I'm just glad that the pastor can lay it out for us so that we don't have to worry about these things ourselves. God has already determined the outcome of the election and soon Thomas Jefferson will lead our country to greatness like his ancestor and namesake, and maybe God will work his magic and make him our president for life and lead us to a new era of enlightenment and greatness, of godliness, and not of the godlessness of the abolitionists."

"If the outcome of the election is already determined why do we even need to bother voting?" Roy said dismissively.

Soon the sermon was over and Roy couldn't help but notice that the majority of people in church had guns at their sides. In fact Charlotte even mentioned why didn't he bring his gun to church and he simply said that he forgot. He always felt that if you had faith in God you shouldn't have to carry a gun with you everywhere you went, and that was coming from him, a police officer.

"Come on let's get the kids, I think we should get home right away," Roy said.

"Don't you want to stay and mingle?" Charlotte asked.

"No I really think that I should get home, I just remembered I had some stuff to do," Roy said.

"What type of stuff?" Charlotte asked.

"Man stuff that your woman brain wouldn't comprehend," Roy shouted trying to control his anger as he was trying to think of an excuse to get out of there as fast as possible.

They went around back and got the children and got them in the car. Roy wanted to talk with their Sunday school teacher but after listening to the sermon earlier he figured that that would kind of be a pointless conversation.

"So what did you kids learn in Sunday school today?" Charlotte asked on the drive home.

"You know just more about how God created the white race to lead everyone and rule over them, much like he created man to rule over women and stuff like that," Atticus said. "You know just stuff about how everyone is happiest when they know their place and don't question God's divine order."

"You kids really believe that," Roy said.

"Of course I do," Bonnie said. "Someday I'm going to meet a

man to take care of me and make babies for him, beautiful pure white babies without a single drop of nigger blood in them so that they will all be pure and godly and morally upright. Isn't that what you want for me daddy?"

"Of course it is dear, of course it is," Roy said as he shook his head before they got home and Roy collapsed onto his bed and looked up at the ceiling. "Heaven help us all," he said as he closed his eyes and went back to sleep.

<u>Chapter 8</u>

It was driving Toby mad that he couldn't stop Master Jefferson and overseer McDonald from abusing Sally. His blood was boiling and he felt like he was going to have a heart attack if he didn't manage to calm himself down somehow. But he also knew that if he tried anything all it would take was one press of a button to potentially give him a fatal shock. Although given the world he found himself in maybe a fatal shock wouldn't necessarily be the worst thing that could possibly happen to him.

"Toby," McDonald said as he smacked Toby to wake him up.

"What is it?" Toby said as he rubbed his eyes, having not slept hardly at all with the thoughts going through his head. As he looked into McDonald's face he didn't see a person, he simply saw some type of disgusting bigoted rapist who he wanted to strangle with all his heart. He even thought that maybe if he acted quickly enough he could get in a shot and disable McDonald and get control of his remote and maybe find some way to escape. But he knew he had to bide his time, now wasn't the time to be foolhardy and get himself killed as that wouldn't benefit him or Sally. He wanted to work out a plan where he could get both of them out of there and as far from this place as possible.

"Master Jefferson wants you to clean his study today so that it looks bright and spotless for when he gives his next interview with the press," McDonald said with a smile. "He said that if you don't do a perfect job I have the obligation to beat you savagely. Personally I hope that you do not do the job to his satisfaction as I am very eager to beat you."

"I'll get right on it," Toby said trying to hold back his anger at being treated as a common house servant.

"See that you do. Cleanliness is next to godliness and that's about as close as heathen savages such as you are going to get to godliness. But this place has to look presentable. Nothing speaks to the efficiency and moral rightness of slavery like a job well done and a house that is immaculately clean. Now get your ass down to the study and you had better be done by the end of the day!"

McDonald took his rubber truncheon and hit Toby on the ass to get him moving down the hall. He didn't know exactly where the study was but figured that he probably should. Luckily he was able to find it quickly enough before McDonald found him and beat him further.

As Toby opened the door to Master Jefferson's study he had to admit that it was an impressive room. There was a desk with giant Confederate flags hanging down from it as well as giant Confederate flags on both sides of it. The desk looked like it was made of ivory or some type of really expensive material.

Toby was immediately struck by a large portrait of what looked like an astronaut on the moon holding up a flag with a swastika on it.

Toby began reading the caption. "In July 1979 man first set foot on the moon for the greater glory of the white race and claimed the moon as property of Nazi Germany. Much as the white race conquered the earth, so too would they conquer the moon and keep it racially pure." Toby shook his head. "I guess on this world Warner Van Braun must have built rockets for the Nazis that eventually got them to the moon."

That was when Toby looked around to see that on every shelf were tons and tons of books and that was when he realized what a fortuitous opportunity this would be for him. Maybe he could find out what the hell was up with this world and how it went so topsy-turvy.

"Working hard Toby?" McDonald said as he walked into the study. "You look like you are idling about; maybe you need a beating in the ass to get you moving."

"I'm working hard," Toby said as he took a rag and began dusting off a large fancy looking globe.

"See that you are, I will be around periodically to check on you to make sure you aren't slacking off, because my job is to make sure you do your job. And if you don't do your job it's my job to beat you senseless. I must say I quite like my job and I really hope that you will give me an excuse to do the most fun part of my job that I look forward to each and every day. Master doesn't like his property to be damaged but a little bit of a beating here and there won't ruin your productivity, in fact it should motivate you to be more productive."

"Don't worry master I am hard at work," Toby said as he dusted the globe really rapidly and forced a smile.

"That's good Toby; a busy nigger is a happy nigger. God put you on the earth to do these types of menial tasks that are beneath white men, so you should take joy in your servitude, it's divinely ordained after all."

"And I thank God every day," Toby said as he put his hand over his heart and pounded his chest.

McDonald looked at him and shook his head. "Crazy nigger," he muttered under his breath as he left the study.

As Toby continued dusting the globe he thought that that was the perfect opportunity to take a look at what the world looked like. He noticed that all of Europe and most of Russia and North Africa had what looked like a swastika over it with the words greater German Reich printed across it.

"I guess on this world the Nazis successfully conquered Europe, Russia and North Africa," he said as he carefully looked at the globe. He turned the globe around to see that there didn't seem to be a Japanese Empire of any kind however.

Toby then turned the globe back to the United States or what he used to know as the United States. It turned out the United States was just a couple of northern states in New England. The Confederate states of America seemed to encompass the entire South, most of the West and parts of Mexico and South America.

He shook his head. "I guess after the South won the Civil War they went on to conquer the West and the North must have stagnated." As he continued looking at the globe he saw that it seemed to be dominated by very few powers. The northern hemisphere seemed to be dominated by the Confederate states where as Europe, Africa and Asia seemed mostly to be under control of the Nazis.

Toby walked around until he saw a larger map of the United States hanging on the wall. Now that he could see it up closer he confirmed his suspicions, the New England area was pretty much all that was left of the United States. Everything south of that was under control of the Confederacy which looked like it had a very expansionist policy. This caused him to frown as he considered his options.

"The North might very well be the last outpost of true democracy and human freedom in a world that is conquered by racist superpowers," he said as he continued staring at the map. As he was staring at the map he heard the door open and turned around to see that McDonald was there so he immediately went back to dusting Master Jefferson's desk.

"Still working Toby?" McDonald said. "Remember I've got my eye on you." He pointed to his eye as he said that. That was the first time that Toby actually noticed but it seemed McDonald had a glass eye and now he was kind of wondering how he managed to get that.

"I guess the life of the slave overseer is a dangerous job, as well it should be," Toby muttered after McDonald left. He didn't have to ask but he could pretty much assume that McDonald had most likely lost that eye in some type of slave confrontation, and he had to admit the thought of him being injured in the line of duty as a slave overseer made him happy. If Toby ever had his way he would lose more than just an eye.

Toby knew that he just had to bide his time but now that McDonald had left he figured he wouldn't be back for a while, so maybe that was a good opportunity for him to take a look at one of the books on the Master's shelves.

"A People's History of the Confederate States of America," Toby said as he took down a large book that seemed to have fancy binding and was probably extremely expensive and seemed to be printed on golden paper.

He decided that he would make sure to dust the bookshelves

while he was looking at the book and just catching casual glances of it.

He started looking through, mostly at the pictures, figuring that he didn't have time to just sit there and casually read a book. What he found was pictures of Abraham Lincoln displayed as a murderous tyrant and sitting on a throne.

Toby couldn't help but notice the important headline that seemed to explain everything. One chapter was titled victory at Gettysburg. He started reading quickly to himself just scanning over it but the main gist of it seemed to be that after the Confederacy had succeeded at Gettysburg the North began a rapid retreat and by 1864 Abraham Lincoln lost reelection and the North sued for peace, even agreed to pay reparations to the south to cover the cost of the war which led to a complete economic collapse of the northern states.

He started glancing around when he noticed another portrait on the wall that looked like the one he saw depicted in the book. It showed a Confederate general signing what looked like the terms of surrender with Abraham Lincoln. He noticed that there were lots of statues of Confederate generals in the master's study. He thought back to that day where he and Roy caught the boy vandalizing the Confederate statues and as he looked at the visage of all the slave owning Confederate generals he felt like vandalizing them himself. The only thing that restrained him was the fact that he knew it would probably cost him his life or something precious to him.

He continued dusting at which point McDonald came in to check up on him.

"How are things coming along Toby?" McDonald said as he peaked into the room.

"I'm just dusting off the statues of the great leaders and founders of our country," he said as he dusted off a statue of Robert E Lee.

"Robert E Lee, truly a great general and a great president," McDonald said.

"Robert E Lee was president," Toby muttered to himself.

McDonald laughed. "You niggers really are dumb; you don't even know who the second president of the Confederacy was. That Robert E Lee, one of the greatest human beings ever to walk the face of the earth. Not only did he lead the Confederacy to victory but afterwards he cleansed the West of those other stinking savages, another member of the mud races, those red skinned Indians."

"They are on reservations now then," Toby said.

McDonald snorted. "What the hell is a reservation? Robert E Lee did the correct thing and he continued expanding westward until every last one of those stinking savages was dead and exterminated from the earth, leaving more room for God's master race, the white race. Don't you niggers know no history?"

"I don't know, being a slave I can't read," Toby said playing dumb.

"Nor should you, a dumb nigger is a happy nigger is an obedient nigger. The more stuff that you know the more dangerous you are."

"I'm kind of interested in history, it was never taught to me and I feel like maybe I would be a better nigger if I knew a little bit about the glorious history of the white race."

McDonald smiled and put his rubber truncheon under Toby's chin and laughed at him.

"What does a nigger like you want to know about the history of the white race?"

Toby shrugged his shoulders, still trying to play dumb. "I guess I just want to know the basics, like how the white race became so superior and managed to conquer all the dumb races like mine."

McDonald smiled. "Okay Toby, I'll amuse you, not because I want to fill your head with knowledge that you are too stupid to comprehend anyway, but because I'm a bit of a history buff myself and I kind of like telling the glorious history of my proud white heritage. My ancestors fought in the Civil War you know, they were heroes of the Confederacy."

"I don't know nothing about my ancestors," Toby said.

"The only thing that you need to know about your ancestors is that they were a bunch of dumb savages like yourself. But I'll tell you why the white race was able to pioneer this country and conquer this nation. There's just something superior in our blood, we have a divine right, a manifest destiny to spread throughout the world and to educate the lower races such as you. Some people call this the white man's burden, and I have to say that's quite accurate. It really is a pain in the ass having to deal with your people Toby. Maybe as a nigger yourself you don't realize how irritating it is for people like me to have to treat you like the idiot children you are and make sure you do your work."

"I'm sorry master McDonald," Toby said as he looked down at his feet and continued dusting Master Jefferson's desk. "I just want to how the white race managed to build this amazing civilization of yours."

"It wasn't easy; it demanded the sacrifice of lots of good decent white people like my ancestors. After we achieved victory over the degenerate North, we spread West, cleansing the world of the heathen Redskin savages and making the entire South free for the expansion of slavery. Then naturally we started conquering the other degenerate races such as the Spaniards. The Confederate states started moving into Mexico and South America and given our natural superiority owing to our bloodlines we naturally were able to achieve victory over them. Sure we used a couple of niggers like yourself as soldiers, disposable people, but lots of useful people, good people, white people, also died fighting for the expansion of this country."

"What about our allies the Germans?"

"The Germans, now there is a hearty bunch of people. The Germans, the one country that is greater than we are and which we aspire to be like. They knew that the white race was naturally superior so they did what was necessary. They rounded up all the Jews and the Bolsheviks and other subversive elements and they got rid of them. They wiped the God damn Russians off the face of the earth, conquered all of Europe and Africa and most of Asia as well. No one is ever going to conquer the Germans."

"What about the North?"

"What about the North?" McDonald said as he took out a cigarette and began smoking and blowing the smoke in Toby's face. "The North is a bunch of backward ass savages. The North hasn't achieved anything worthwhile since their defeat in the Civil War. But the North, the United States as they still call themselves, they are weak and pathetic, and that is because of people like yourself Toby.

Do you know that in the North things are crazy and all topsy-turvy? They allow the races to mix, can you believe that? Up north they actually have Blacks and whites mixing their genetics, polluting the white genetic line. That's why people up north will never be great like the Confederate states down south or the greater German Reich. The North is a bunch of decadent scum, non-Christian, a mix of races and religions, dominated by socialists, Jews and other crazy people. You know in the north they actually allow dumb niggers like yourself to vote, and women too! Luckily we live down here in the South where they suppressed all of those horrific movements like suffragettes, abolitionists, secularists, trade unionists and other scum of the earth. That's all that you will find up north."

Toby smiled. At least in some part of the world, however small, there was some last refuge for freedom, some last chance for him, some possibility of hope. And failing that he figured that Canada was probably still intact because it appeared on the map as its own independent nation. But the United States, even if it was defeated in the Civil War, it still existed.

"What are you smiling about boy?" McDonald said as he poked Toby in the chest with his rubber truncheon. "You're not getting any type of idiot ideas of trying to escape up north are you? I know that lots of niggers is stupid and think that they can get up north, go to that lousy socialist shithole known as the United States run by a God damn Bolshevik Jew from their capital city of New York. Their country lets everyone in, escaped slaves, foreigners, nonwhites, non-Christians. There's no state church. Trust me, you're best to stay here in the South where people know their places and live by the sweat of their brow. And if you get any crazy ideas about going up north just remember all I need is one press of a button and you will be on the floor shitting yourself to death and convulsing. You understand that Toby?"

"Yes master sir, I would never want to leave the glorious South," Toby said not having to fake a smile because now that he knew that the North provided some type of potential refuge for people like him, a safe place where he could live freely.

"Why are you smiling so big again?"

"It's the audacity of hope," Toby said smirking.

McDonald got right up in his face and looked at him with his one eye raised. "What the God damn hell is the audacity of hope?"

"Have you ever heard of Barack Obama?"

"What kind of crazy ass nigger name is that?" McDonald shook his head. "Just get your ass back to work. And this conversation we just had, it never fucking took place, got it." McDonald hit him hard in the stomach with his rubber truncheon.

"I understand master," Toby said as he continued polishing things. "I really love my work."

Toby spent the rest of the day just focusing on his work and didn't try to sneak anymore peeks at any type of history book. Just knowing that the North, that the United States that he knew and loved, still existed out there was all he really needed to know. The rest of the world may have been under the jackboot of white supremacist tyranny, but as long as the United States existed there was still some hope left in the world.

When he had finished doing his work he was quite exhausted, and when McDonald had seen that he had done the job to his specifications that was when he was sent back to his quarters where he saw Sally, who for some reason was walking around completely naked.

"Sally, why are you naked?" Toby asked. He could see that she was clearly uncomfortable and did not seem to be naked by choice.

"The master prefers to see me this way," Sally said. "Says he likes to see me humiliated, he said without clothing maybe I would be more submissive and obedient."

Toby wanted to say something to her, wanted to tell her that she didn't have to do whatever the master wanted, but he knew that for now that wasn't true. He may have had hope now but he still didn't know how he was going to get out of there. And he also felt guilty because he also couldn't help but find Sally rather attractive in that state and he had to control himself.

"Sally get your naked black nigger ass over here, the master wants to see you," McDonald said as he waved her over.

"I have to go," Sally said with a frown as she touched her eye which Toby just noticed looked swollen. He was so shocked at seeing Sally naked like that that he hadn't even noticed that it looked like she had a black eye.

Toby wanted to tell her to stop; he wanted to pull her away knowing what the master was most likely about to do to her. But once again he felt the collar around his neck and realized that there was nothing he could do.

"I guess you had better go then," he said as he waved to Sally, gritted his teeth and decided then and there that he was going to begin planning his escape up north. He didn't know how he was going to do it, he didn't know if he would succeed, but with God as his witness he was going to try if it killed him, and he was going to bring Sally with him.

<u>Chapter 9</u>

The rest of the week was uneventful where Roy tried the best he could to do his job even though he was growing increasingly sick with himself for the fact that most of his job entailed brutalizing people of color. Sure he had to deal with white criminals as well, but the overwhelming focus of his job was hunting down potential escaped slaves and subversives like abolitionists. He felt less like a cop and more like a Gestapo officer because he now lived in a totalitarian state.

"How was your day dear?" Charlotte asked with a big smile as she put dinner on the table.

"You know the usual," Roy said. By the usual it meant that frequently people would call just because a black person was walking around outside minding their own business. When a person saw a black person sometimes they would automatically assume that it was an escaped slave and they would call it in and the police would have to investigate and check his papers. But even free blacks, who were a minority, tended to keep their heads down and tried not to be noticed as much as most people naturally assumed them to be slaves.

"By the usual you mean dealing with niggers all day," Charlotte said.

"Yes something like that," Roy said. "I mean my God Charlotte sometimes people in this town so much as see an African-

American walking the streets freely and they call the police as though he were a criminal."

"A what American?"

"An African-American." He looked at Charlotte who gave him a baffled look as though she didn't comprehend what he was saying. That was when he realized that he had not heard that term ever since he arrived in this new reality. "You know niggers." He cringed every time he said that word and he was starting to understand how Toby must have felt whenever he heard it.

Charlotte shook her head. "African-American, what a crazy term, people from Africa certainly aren't Americans, and people probably should call in when they see a nigger walking across the street. The fact is that the majority of them are slaves and if they are out walking freely they could be trying to escape. And you know that most of the crime in this country is the result of niggers."

"I prefer not to talk about work once I get home," Roy said as he sat down at the dinner table.

Charlotte shook her head. "I'm sorry dear I forgot that work is often unpleasant and having to deal with niggers all day I can't blame you for not wanting to hear more about niggers when you get home."

That was when Atticus came into the room with a big smile on his face.

"There's mommy's little nigger killer!" Charlotte said as she kissed Atticus.

"Charlotte!" Roy shouted struggling to contain his anger. "How was school today son?"

"We learned all about World War II and how the Nazis burned down the Vatican making the world safe for the one true form of Christianity, white Protestant," Atticus said with a smile. "Isn't it great that the Nazis got rid of the Papists?"

Roy was once again beginning to feel sick as his child seemed to be celebrating a religious-based genocide.

"They didn't get rid of all of them son," Charlotte said. "There are still people out there who call themselves Catholics, especially up north in the United States. That's going to be the downfall of their country, letting Catholics and Jews not just have the right to exist, but to actually have the right to vote and hold office! I mean can you even imagine?"

Atticus smiled. "History is my favorite class, it's where we learn all about how great the white race is and how we have triumphed over all of the degenerate races of the world to make ourselves the master race. Dad I think when I get older I want to go to study in Germany."

"We'll see son, that is still many years away," Roy said as his stomach began to turn and he started losing his appetite.

"Germany is a beautiful country," Charlotte said. "It's basically the world capital. Maybe he could even visit the capital city of Germania and learn all about the history of the creation of the Nazi state. I think it's important for the children to get a broader education. By studying Nazi Germany Atticus can come home and use what he has learned there to help make our America, the true America, great like Germany, unlike those decadent United States. Long live the Confederacy!"

"Long live the Confederacy!" Atticus and Bonnie said together as they raised their forks.

"Yes the Confederacy is great," Roy said trying to feign enthusiasm.

"Dad since tomorrow is Saturday do you think I could go out with my friends?" Atticus asked.

"I guess so, did you do your homework?" Roy asked as he ate some of his chicken.

"I already did it," Atticus said. "Like I said history is my favorite subject and the history of Nazi Germany is my favorite history of all."

"Even more exciting than the history of the founding of the Confederacy?" Bonnie asked. "I always found the most exciting part of history is when Lincoln surrendered and walked away in shame realizing that his tyranny would never stand."

"The defeat of Lincoln was pretty great, but the rise of Hitler was even more exciting," Atticus said. "Hitler was an even better leader than Robert E Lee and Jefferson Davis."

"What do you think dear; who do you think was the better leader?" Charlotte said. "Robert E Lee and Jefferson Davis were true great Confederate Americans; our country wouldn't even exist without them. But that Adolf Hitler, he really knows how to inspire a nation to great things. I wish that we had leaders like that today. I am hoping that Thomas Jefferson though will help to make this country great again and crack down on all of the nigger revolts and slave rebellions."

"Where did you want to go out with your friends son?" Roy asked.

"My friend got tickets to one of the nigger fights, just like the ones you see on TV!" Atticus said his face brimming with excitement.

"Wow he got tickets to the nigger fights?" Bonnie asked. "You're so lucky; I want to see a nigger fight as well."

"Can I go dad?" Atticus said with a huge smile.

"I don't know, all that violence isn't necessarily a good thing," Roy said disgusted at the very idea of "nigger fights" as everyone called them.

"Yeah but it's not like any actual people are getting hurt, just niggers and slaves, as if there's a difference between those two things," Atticus said as he began laughing along with Bonnie.

"Dear, Atticus has already killed his first nigger, I think he's old enough to go to one of the nigger fights," Charlotte said.

"I'll think about it," Roy said. "Now let's just have dinner peacefully without talking anymore about niggers."

"We forgot to say grace!" Charlotte said.

"I'll say grace," Atticus said as he folded his hands in prayer. "Dear God we thank you for this food that we are about to receive and please protect us all and to protect and glorify the white race and the true believers against all the enemies of the faith, Amen."

"Let's eat!" Bonnie said as the family began digging into the food.

Roy got up from the table.

"What's the matter dear?" Charlotte asked.

"I guess I'm just not that hungry," Roy said not wanting to admit that he felt like he was going to be sick. This wasn't the family that he knew and he didn't know exactly what had happened to them and he feared what the answer might be.

Toby was woken up by a grinning McDonald.

"Do you want to know why I am smiling Toby?" McDonald asked as he smiled with his big ugly yellow teeth.

"I'm guessing probably not," Toby said.

"Master Jefferson has chosen you as his chosen competitor in the nigger fights."

"What are the nigger fights?"

McDonald laughed. "What are the nigger fights, I know that you're a dumb nigger but you should know what the nigger fights are. You're going to be fighting in gladiatorial combat for the greater glory of Master Jefferson and you had better win because he has a lot of money riding on this event."

"What happens if I lose?"

McDonald began laughing again.

"What's so funny?" Toby asked feeling more nervous by the second.

"Well nigger fights are generally to the death, if you lose you will be dead," McDonald said as he laughed heartily. "So eat a good breakfast this morning Toby, it might be your last."

McDonald ran off laughing like a hyena as Toby just sat there shaking his head. "Christ and I thought Trump's America sucked," Toby said under his breath.

Toby got out of bed and started eating his bacon like he did every morning. He didn't find the bacon very appetizing but he figured if he was going to be fighting to the death he would probably need his strength. That was when he saw Sally walking around, once again still limping and still completely naked.

"Hi Sally," Toby said. "How are you today?" He felt it was a dumb question the moment he asked it because she was obviously not doing very well.

"Every day is the same for a nigger Toby," Sally said. "I heard that master Jefferson is going to take you down to the nigger fights today. I'll be praying to God for your safe return."

"Thank you Sally," Toby said. He didn't even know what to say in a situation like this. Here he was in an entirely insane world. He was talking to a naked slave woman who was clearly being sexually and physically abused, he was eating what could be his final breakfast before going to a gladiatorial fight to the death, and he still didn't know how on earth he found himself in this insane situation.

"Come on Toby, it's time for your meeting with destiny," McDonald said as he could see that McDonald was looking at Sally and licking his lips. The very thought of that infuriated him. That was when he knew that no matter what happened he had to survive today because without him there he didn't know exactly what would happen to Sally. He still didn't know how to get them free but he knew that he was the only hope that Sally had of ever escaping to freedom, even if she didn't know that.

"Goodbye Sally," Toby said as he waved to her as she just smiled and nodded. He wasn't sure if he would ever see her again but he wanted to get one last good look at her if this was going to be the day he died.

"I can't believe I'm really going to see the nigger fights!" Atticus shouted as they arrived at the arena.

"Your dad actually let you go," Tommy said.

"Of course he did, my dad catches slaves and niggers for a living, why would he be upset by this," Atticus said, not wanting to admit that his father didn't give him permission and he told his father that he was going to an event down at the church. "Although lately my dad has been acting strange."

"Strange how?" Tommy asked.

"I don't know ever since I killed that nigger, the escaped slave who came into our backyard, he has been looking at me like there was something wrong with me."

"You killed your first nigger; he's probably just shocked at how fast you are growing up. My father realizes that you are a hero and thinks that you're probably going to have your father's job one day."

"I certainly hope so. I'm hoping that when I graduate from high school that maybe I can go to college and study abroad in Nazi Germany, to learn how they really get things done. I really wish our country was more like Nazi Germany. But it seems like lately my dad just doesn't want to hear any mention of niggers."

"Well he doesn't know what he's missing," Tommy said as they gave their tickets at the front.

"You boys get your seats, I'm going to go get us some snacks," Tommy's dad said as the two of them got up in the front row.

"Ladies and gentlemen, boys and girls, welcome to the world's most popular sport, nigger fights!" the announcer said as the room filled up with all kinds of bright lights. "The World Nigger Fight Federation has sponsored this event and a portion of the proceeds will be going to the families of the victims of escaped slaves and abolitionists."

Everyone in the audience began cheering.

"Tonight we have a very special match as tonight's competitor is a slave owned by Gov. Jefferson himself and he is hoping to use the proceeds from this as part of a fundraiser for his run for president so that he can make this country great again."

People in the audience began roaring and cheering as they started waving all sorts of Confederate flags around.

"The thing that really sucks about a lot of these fights is that sometimes they let the niggers free," Atticus said. "Can you believe that they would actually let niggers go free and mingle amongst normal decent God-fearing white people? It sick, it's why my dad's job is so terrible."

Tommy shook his head. "It is pretty terrible but maybe if Gov. Jefferson becomes President he will change that. At least even a free black man is only allowed to have so much money and has to give the rest of the state, the freedman's tax, so they don't get too uppity. So even if one of these slaves does get freed they will still be living in poverty."

"Yeah but a nigger living in poverty is extremely dangerous," Atticus said. "Sometimes I think that we should just kill all of them."

"Yeah but we need them for slaves," Tommy said. "Although my dad says that some of the problems of unemployment is because slave labor doesn't cost anything as people would rather buy slaves than hire poor whites to do the work."

"Now you're starting to sound like an abolitionist."

"Hey you take that back, you know I'm no traitor to this

country. It's just a fact that slavery takes away a lot of jobs from poor white people. I certainly don't think we should abolish slavery, I'm just saying that white people need jobs too. White lives matter."

"They certainly matter a lot more than the lives of niggers."

"Well we can certainly both agree to that," the two of them said as they laughed as the fight began starting.

"In this corner we have fighting for Gov. Jefferson, Toby," the announcer said as Toby walked into the arena in what looked like a gladiator outfit. A metal plate on his chest and what looked like brass knuckles on his hands.

"Yea Toby!" Atticus shouted as he waved his little Confederate flag. "Win this one for Gov. Jefferson!"

"And in the corner, fighting for master Reynolds is Willy," the announcer said as another black man came onto the stage similarly attired to Toby but looking older and not quite as physically fit.

"This hardly seems like a fair fight," Tommy said. "I'm starting to think that maybe this is rigged to make Gov. Jefferson look well."

"Now you're starting to sound like an abolitionist again," Atticus said.

The bell rang and the fight began with Toby and Willy circling around each other making punching motions. Although he was a police officer Toby felt nervous as he had never been in a fight like this before. He did a little bit of boxing in college but that wasn't quite the same as fighting to the death.

"Come here you stupid nigger," Willy said as he smiled and licked his lips revealing that he had been missing several teeth.

"What the fuck," Toby said under his breath. Who was this crazy old coot?

Toby started moving back as he did not want to hurt this man who was clearly elderly and infirm. In fact as Toby watched this man circling around him he realized that he should easily be able to defeat him with a couple of blows. But Toby did not want to take the life of an innocent old man like that.

"Come on Toby clobber him!" Atticus shouted from the front row as he waved his Confederate flag around. Toby heard Atticus's voice and it sounded vaguely familiar to him but he couldn't really distinguish it over all the shouting and cheering.

"Come on nigger," Willy said as he made a few swipes at Toby. "You're not so strong."

"Kill him Toby!" Atticus shouted again.

Toby was distracted by the familiar sound of Atticus's voice and that's when Willy got a couple of blows in causing Toby to fall backwards as people started making all sorts of ooing and ahing noises. Toby tried to look around in the audience as to where the sound of Atticus's voice was coming from. He knew that he had heard that voice somewhere before but he couldn't quite place it.

"I'm going to kill you nigger!" Willy said as he started charging towards Toby who ducked down and used his brass knuckles to hit Willy right square in the balls causing him to yell in pain and fall back a bit grabbing himself. Toby didn't like to fight dirty but the move was instinctive and it was over before he had even realized what he had done.

Willy started circling around and Toby took a few more swipes at him hitting him on the arms and once on the face causing blood to come out of his nose.

"Kill him!" people in the audience began shouting until it became loud droning chanting that drowned out all other sounds.

"I'm not going to kill an old man," Toby said under his breath as he looked at Willy who looked increasingly dizzy and was bleeding all over the place.

"Remember the rules of the game, if a competitor fails to kill his opponent both opponents will be put to death," the announcer shouted.

Toby was taken aback by that announcement and was momentarily distracted when all the sudden he heard a loud screaming and he turned around to see Willy coming right at him. Without even thinking he put up his fist slamming it right in Willy's face causing Willy to go falling right on his back.

"Kill him!" everyone in the audience began shouting as they continued waving around their Confederate flags and looking increasingly bloodthirsty.

"Kill the motherfucking nigger!" an elderly man in the

audience said as he jumped up and down.

Toby refused to give into the bloodlust of the crowd and he stood there as what looked like a referee came out, kneeled down and felt Willy's pulse before holding up his hand.

"The winner of the match is Toby!" the referee shouted as everyone began cheering. "Congratulations to Gov. Thomas Jefferson for his victory today."

Toby began to feel sick. In all his years as a police officer he had never killed anyone in the line of duty, and now here he was, purely by accident and in self-defense, he killed an innocent old man, most likely a lifelong slave who had never known the sweet taste of freedom and had probably been trained to hate his own kind.

Toby couldn't help but fight back tears at the thought of what he had done. He wanted to shout something to the audience but he knew that he wouldn't be heard over all the cheering and shouting.

"You're free now Willy," Toby said as he fought back tears.

"Atticus what the hell are you doing here?!" Roy said as he grabbed Atticus by the arm.

"Dad, what are you doing here?" Atticus said realizing that he was going to be in a whole lot of trouble.

"Your sister said that you went to the nigger fights even though you knew I explicitly told you that you couldn't come."

"That little snitch! Dad I just wanted to see some niggers fight each other. I see them on TV all the time. Hell dad I've killed a nigger of my own."

"You are in big trouble mister, and we are going home right now," Roy said as he dragged Atticus out of the arena.

Toby felt numb as he stood up there on the stage as people cheered the fact that he just brutally killed an elderly old man, who clearly never had a chance against someone as physically fit and young as he was. He could hear that Thomas Jefferson was giving some type of a speech about his own victory but the words went right in and out of his ear.

As Toby wiped away his tears he looked off in the distance and that was when he saw it. He saw Roy dragging Atticus out of the arena.

"Roy," Toby shouted as he tried waving to Roy but Roy had

his back turned towards him and certainly couldn't hear what he was saying. "Roy!" he shouted again but it was too late as Roy had already left the arena.

"Three cheers for Gov. Jefferson and his fighting slave Toby and Long live the Confederacy!" the announcer said as everyone began cheering and all sorts of lights and smoke filled the room until Toby could no longer see Roy.

Toby thought that he would get to say something but he was just dragged off the stage as he watched people drag off the corpse of Willy, probably to throw him in some type of unmarked grave.

That was when Toby noticed something. He hadn't even thought of it but they had removed his collar and this could be his chance to escape.

"Well nigger it's time to go home," he heard McDonald say as he felt the collar go back around his neck. "Looks like you get to live another day, lucky you. But I guess lucky me too, as I would miss not getting the chance to beat you regularly you vicious killer, you animal."

Toby wanted to shout at McDonald but he realized that he had already lost his chance. Once again he was shackled and he couldn't even refute what McDonald had told him. From that day forward Toby would have to live with the fact that he was a killer and he was still not yet free.

Chapter 10

"Atticus I specifically forbade you from going to the nigger fights!" Roy said as he dragged Atticus through the front door.

"What's the matter?" Charlotte said.

"Atticus went off to go to the nigger fights despite the fact that I explicitly forbade him from going," Roy said.

"I don't see what's wrong about going to nigger fights, we watch them on TV all the time, seeing them up close isn't that much different is it?" Charlotte asked.

"I just don't approve of nigger fights in general," Roy said shaking his head.

"Or maybe you're just going soft on niggers!" Atticus shouted as he pointed at his father. "You know lately dad, ever since

I killed that slave, you've been acting really weird, you're almost sounding like an abolitionist sometimes."

"You have been acting strange lately dear," Charlotte said. "It is almost like you're an entirely different person or something like that."

"I'm just under a real lot of stress at work," Roy said. "That is why when I tell you that you cannot do something I expect you to listen to me."

"I just wanted to go out there to support Gov. Jefferson, he's going to be our future President someday," Atticus said shaking his head. "Don't you want Thomas Jefferson to be the next president of the Confederacy?"

"A boy your age shouldn't be concerned with politics, you can't even vote yet," Roy said shaking his head.

"Of course not, I don't own any slaves, only slave-owners can vote," Atticus said. "It ensures that only property owning people who have contributed to the country have any say in the running of the country. Maybe if you would get some slaves we could actually have some say in the way this country is heading because it's going to hell in a hand basket."

"Atticus just go to your room," Roy said as he pointed to Atticus's room as Atticus walked off sulking with a frown on his face.

"You should be happy that our son is so politically engaged, most people his age aren't as concerned with the fate of the country," Charlotte said. "And he should be, his father is the head slave catcher around here. I think he's just concerned for your safety. With President Clifton being so soft on the nigger riots and the abolitionist terrorism it makes things more dangerous out there for you. That is why we all have to hope that Gov. Jefferson becomes the next president and sets things right."

"I don't even know if I want to be a slave catcher anymore," Roy said. That was technically a lie; he knew very well that he did not want to be a slave catcher anymore.

"What are you saying?" Charlotte said as she looked at him horrified. "Are you saying that you want to quit your job?"

Roy shook his head. "I don't know what I want to do right

now Charlotte."

"But if you quit your job how will you support this family? I'm used to living the good life."

"Sometimes it's not right to be living the good life at the expense of other people."

"What other people? You're not talking about niggers, are you? Please tell me that you're not developing sympathies for the abolitionists. Here, maybe you should listen to the inspiring speech of Gov. Jefferson on the campaign trail."

Charlotte turned on the television where Gov. Jefferson was smiling and giving a major speech.

"My fellow Confederate Americans," Gov. Jefferson said at his podium which had a Confederate flag draped over it as it seemed large numbers of people in the audience were similarly waving Confederate flags and swastika flags. "We live in troubled times, divisive times. When our country should be unified under the banner of slavery, we have abolitionists who want to divide this country, who want to set Negro slaves free to walk about and rape and murder white women. They want to free our entire labor force which the entire economy is based on. We have an economy based on slavery, the most glorious institution ever devised of by mankind. Slavery has been practiced by every great civilization going back to antiquity. You might even say that civilization itself is founded on the slavery of the lesser races, of the weak and the stupid. The only natural order is the domination of the weak and the stupid by the superior race, by people who are racially pure and have an unpolluted gene line. All of our founding fathers were slave owners, my namesake and ancestor, the great Thomas Jefferson who wrote the Declaration of Independence, owned slaves. We fought an entire Civil War to maintain the institution of slavery. But God was on our side in that war and that led to the triumph of the Confederacy and the white race.

"Now you have people who want to undermine our most sacred institution. You have people who want to give rights to uneducated slaves, even want to permit interbreeding between the races, who want to destroy our economic system and to go around waving flags of the United States, an act that is extremely illegal. In fact you even have abolitionists burning the Confederate flag and vandalizing Confederate monuments! If you ask me abolitionism is a mental illness. You've actually got abolitionists promoting this idea that the earth is getting warmer. Even if it were, which as we all know is just a Zionist plot to undermine our economic institutions, so what; a warmer world is a better world.

"These abolitionists want to up end every social order and every form of morality. It is only natural for the strong to conquer the weak. The white race pioneered this country and they defeated the weak and lazy Indians, who were primitive savages practicing a pagan faith. In the same way that we pioneered this country by wiping out the lesser races, our allies in Germany, the Nazis, successfully managed to conquer Europe, Asia and Africa because they were part of the master race. We wouldn't have life so good if it weren't for the slavery of the lower races of the world. Every white person owes their existence to the fact that the Orientals, the niggers and the other lesser races are where they currently belong, working in factories and fields to provide food and merchandise for you at affordable prices. As every educated person knows the natural order is white over black, man over woman and powerful over the weak.

"The Nazis have created a slave empire on par with ancient Rome and Greece and working with our allies in Nazi Germany we hope that we can transform these Confederate states into an empire as great as the Nazi Reich, an empire that will hopefully last for 1000 years. I say let us see the Confederacy last for a 1000 years as well, in glory. That is why I encourage every property owning white Christian male to do their patriotic duty and protect our nation by voting for me and The Southern Heritage Party and let's make our country great again. I say slavery today, slavery tomorrow, and slavery forever! God bless the Confederacy!"

Roy turned off the television. "I think that I've had enough of that for one night."

Toby was so glad to be home and to still be alive until he remembered where he lived and what his life was like now. He still couldn't get the fact that he had seen Roy out of his mind.

"Toby you're alive!" Sally said as she limped towards him.

"It's good to see that you are okay."

"But I'm not okay Sally, not the least little bit," Toby said shaking his head.

"What's the matter Toby?"

Toby practically wanted to shout but he maintained his composure. "What's the matter? What's the matter? This whole world is what's the matter Sally. I just was forced to fight a man to the death, an elderly feeble man. I had never taken a life before, not even in several years on the police force."

"What are you talking about Toby? You know that niggers can't be police officers. The job of police officers is to control niggers like us."

"Stop using that word," Toby said. "We are not niggers; we are Americans, African-Americans. And we shouldn't be slaves either. Do you think that Martin Luther King, Malcolm X, Rosa Parks and Barack Obama would stand for this?"

"Toby you're not making any sense. If the master hears you talking like that he will punish you, give you a whipping. Why are you saying all these things?"

"I have a dream Sally. I dream someday of a world where all men and women can be free to pursue their own destiny. I have a dream of a world where little black boys and little black girls can go to school together without prejudice, a world where people are judged by the content of their character and not by the color of their skin. A world full of hope and change we can believe in!"

"Toby I don't understand."

Toby shook his head. "No of course you don't, you grew up in a different world than the one that I grew up in, a world with things like the Emancipation Proclamation, the civil rights movement, the million Man March, BlackLivesMatter. I came from a world where I was a police officer, where we were free, where we had a black president. Oh it wasn't perfect, in fact things were steadily getting worse in many ways, but nothing was as bad as this. No man, woman or child on the face of the earth should have to live the way we live, where people own other people and can do whatever they want to them. For God's sake Sally look at you, you're naked and bruised and you are standing there acting like this is normal."

"Well well well well surviving a brush with death has made one a pretty uppity nigger today," McDonald said as he walked into the room brandishing a whip.

"He didn't mean anything master McDonald," Sally said.

"The hell he didn't, I'm going to beat some sense into this lunatic," McDonald said as he started stroking his whip with a smile on his face.

"Bring it on motherfucker," Toby said. At this point he didn't care if he died. At least if he died now he would die standing up for something like all those great civil rights leaders he had read about and looked up to, that inspired him to become a police officer so he could be one of the good cops so sorely needed.

McDonald went to raise his whip when all of the sudden there was a loud booming explosion in the sky and suddenly all of the lights in the mansion started exploding and the power went out, leaving the room dark.

"What the fuck?" McDonald said but before he could say another word he felt someone knocking him to the ground. It was Toby choking him to death.

"Toby what are you doing, you'll kill him!" Sally shouted.

"Well at least I'll be killing someone who had it coming this time," Toby said as he continued choking McDonald.

"You God damned nigger," McDonald said as he spit in Toby's face.

"Say that word one last time, because it will be your last!"

"Nigger!" McDonald said before Toby snapped his neck.

Toby immediately stood up shocked at what he had done but now he knew that there was no going back.

"Sally come with me," Toby said.

"Go with you where?" Sally said. "Toby I'm afraid. What's happening?"

"This is our chance Sally; we can escape up north, to freedom. I can't promise you that it's going to be perfect. I know that even up north there is a lot of resentment and hatred towards us, but we would be free Sally. We wouldn't have to work for Master Jefferson anymore and he would no longer be able to hurt and abuse you."

"Toby I'm afraid," Sally said as she hugged him.

"Don't be, I will protect you," Toby said. "I swear on my life and I swear to God that I won't let any more harm ever come to you ever again. Do you trust me?"

As Toby was standing there looking at Sally, that was when a bunch of people broke in to the room brandishing guns. Toby was frightened for a moment until he realized that the people holding the guns were black just like him.

"Greetings brother, the revolution has begun!" the leader of the group said as he adjusted his bandanna. "Now come with me to freedom!"

As Toby and Sally ran behind this leader and his band of men firing guns in all directions they noticed that behind them the governor's mansion was burning to the ground and he stopped and turned to look at it.

"Beautiful isn't it, cracker ass motherfuckers," the leader said as he put his arms around Toby and Sally.

Toby had no idea who this revolutionary leader was, all he knew was that he liked him, he liked him a lot, and he knew that he was going to follow him wherever he happened to be going.

"Burn baby burn," he said as he, Sally and the rest of the slaves from Gov. Jefferson's mansion ran off as it burned behind them, the first of many bridges that they would have to burn on their path to freedom.

Chapter 11

Roy was attempting to sleep when he heard a knock at his door. He answered it and there was officer Buford.

"What's going on, it's the middle of the night?" Roy said as he yawned.

"Didn't you realize that the power's down. It was a terrorist attack!" Buford said shaking his head. "A bunch of those God damned abolitionists had something called an EMP pulse weapon. They were trying to disrupt the election coming up next week, knocked out the entire power grid across the entire state. Now all the slaves are running free and rioting. Gov. Jefferson said that every officer should be called up as this is a national emergency and he has declared martial law. Luckily we had several ways of communication there were EMP protected."

"Daddy what's the matter," Atticus said as he got out of bed. "Are there niggers going around hurting people?"

"Go back to bed Atticus, this doesn't concern you," Roy said shaking his head.

"Normally I wouldn't be saying this but maybe you should give your child a gun," Buford said. "We know he's a good shot with niggers, aren't you boy?"

"What's going on?" Charlotte said as she came out of the bedroom still in her nightgown, her Confederate flag nightgown.

"Charlotte I want you to keep the kids inside, we are under a national emergency here. I want you all to stay in the house and whatever you do don't open the door unless it is me. If you have to take one of the guns out and stand guard but I have to go do my duty and reestablish order."

"What's going on daddy?" Bonnie asked.

"Kids just stay inside with your mother, I love you both but right now I have a job to do," Roy said.

"I want to help to protect against the niggers dad," Atticus said.

"Atticus you are to stay here and to do whatever your mother says. You have to protect your mother and sister and you can do that best by staying here. Do you understand?"

"But dad –" Atticus began saying.

"Not another word or I will ground you for the rest of your natural life, do you understand?"

"I understand dad, I'll protect them," Atticus said as he nodded.

"Come on let's get in the squad car, I will drive," Buford said as Roy got his gun, put on his uniform and got in the squad car. "Fortunately the squad car is protected against EMP attacks, God bless the governor for putting that bill through. Luckily we also have the slave database that is backed up as it was meant to survive a nuclear war. Unfortunately the microchips aren't working so it's not going to be easy to track down the slaves but right now they are all over the place."

Roy began looking through the digital slave database on the squad car's computer and that was when he saw a familiar face. "Toby," Roy said as he saw Toby's face looking back at him.

"You recognize that nigger?" Buford asked. "Well if you see him, shoot first, ask questions later."

"Our jobs as police officers aren't just to go around shooting niggers indiscriminately," Roy said.

"You're not one of all those nigger lives matter people are you?"

"Nigger lives matter?"

"You know that movement by slave-owners, the argument being that niggers are valuable property and that by shooting them you are costing the slave-owners money. The slave-owners feel that if we shoot their niggers when they are being disobedient that they should be reimbursed by the state. Fortunately the governor thinks that is a load of crap as if you can't control your slaves you should have to pay the penalty for their disobedience. This is a national emergency so we are authorized to use any means necessary. If you see a black person out on the street they should be presumed dangerous and they should be shot. Maybe we will even get to try out our new sonic deterrent weapon."

"Sonic deterrent weapon?"

"Yeah we have this new weapon that when fired at a large group or a large crowd of protesters or other subversives, like escaped slaves, the blast of sound is enough to knock them down and even cause brain hemorrhages. We can thank our friends in the Nazi Reich for that. It's brand-new, it's an excellent weapon of mass death. I can't wait to start killing niggers with it. In fact here are a couple right now."

"Maybe we shouldn't be so quick to use this new destructive weapon."

"Fuck that," Buford said as he pressed a button as a horde of escaped slaves in front of them grabbed their heads and started screaming. "Now that was fun! This is why I love my job."

As Roy looked around him he saw that the city had gone completely dark except for the fires that were burning in every direction, most of which seemed to be electrical in nature but, others that seemed to be deliberately set by the rioting slaves. He also saw burning Confederate flags and what looked like a toppled statue of Robert E Lee.

"I think that we should get out and start scouting around," Buford said. "Cover me."

Buford got out of the squad car and no sooner than he had done so was he hit with a hail of bullets. Luckily the bulletproof glass of the squad car protected Roy from being hit by the machine gun fire but now he saw that his squad car was surrounded.

Roy could hear car alarms going off in every direction as well as the sound of explosions. As he looked around he could see that he was now surrounded by a bunch of angry looking black men holding machine guns, crowbars and torches.

"Well I guess this is how I die," Roy said as he looked into the eye of the leader of the gang and suddenly recognized him. It was Toby. Toby came around to the squad car and looked in the window and looked Roy right in the eye.

"Roy?" Toby asked.

Roy picked up the intercom and started talking. "Toby?"

"You know this cracker ass motherfucker," said Elijah, the revolutionary leader who had freed them from the governor's mansion.

"I think I do, or at least I did know him, I don't know if he is the same person," Toby said.

"It's me Toby, it's Roy, your old friend and partner," Roy said over the intercom.

"Were you lovers or something?" Elijah asked shaking his head. "Because you know that shit's illegal."

"Not where I came from," Toby said shaking his head. "But no we we're totally not lovers. I was a police officer with him."

"Nigger you is crazy," Elijah said.

"Don't hurt him," Toby said. "Roy come out of the car and I promise that we will not hurt you."

"I'd like to believe you Toby but there seem to be a large number of men with machine guns surrounding my vehicle," Roy said. He was tempted to press the button to deploy the sonic dispersal unit but he knew if he had done that he would end up harming Toby. And after everything he saw he knew that whatever was going on, he was on the same side as Toby.

Very slowly Roy got out of the squad car and put his hands up.

"Let's kill this motherfucker," Elijah said as he pointed his gun at Roy but Toby got in between them.

"Nobody's going to hurt this man," Toby said. "He is a good man, I know him."

"Do you know that he is slave catcher general," Elijah said.

"I officially quit," Roy said.

"Easy to say that now that your life is in danger," Elijah said.

Toby looked at Roy. "Can you prove to me that you are the Roy that I know?"

Roy looked at Toby with tears in his eyes. "Toby, it's me it's Roy. Fine, I voted for Trump, although after seeing this I kind of wished that I had voted for Obama. I get it now, I was wrong."

"Who the fuck is this cracker talking about?" Elijah said.

"The first black president of the United States of America," Toby said shaking his head. "As well as the first orange president, it's a long story."

"You're one crazy ass nigger," Elijah said shaking his head.

"Roy do you think you can get some friends of mine to the border?" Toby asked as he pointed to Sally who seemed to be dressed in stolen clothing that still had the tags on it.

"Why do you want to go to the border?" Roy asked.

"Because that is where freedom is. There is a free land up north. The United States that we used to know, it's not the same place, but it still exists. Please Roy, if I stay here I will almost certainly be killed or sent back into slavery. If you drive us around like you had captured us we might be able to get to the border before anyone notices."

"Do you think that they will actually let you across the border wall," Elijah said.

"Border wall?" Roy asked.

"Yeah you know that Gov. Jefferson erected around the northern border to keep the slaves from escaping, wanted the United

States to pay for it," Elijah said.

"Well I guess there are some similarities to the world we came from," Toby said. "But do you think you can do it Roy?"

Roy nodded. "Get in; I'll take you to the border. I don't know what I'm going to do when I get there. I still have family back here, although I don't know if they are the family that I know and love."

"Come on Sally, let's escape to freedom," Toby said as he and Sally got into the squad car.

"Freedom," Sally said as though it were an incomprehensible word.

"Let's get the hell out of here," Roy said as they started driving away from the burning remains of their home of Charlottesville as they made their way to the border and hopefully to freedom.

<u>Epilogue</u>

Roy didn't know exactly what to say to Toby and Toby didn't know exactly what to say to Roy. They both knew that something crazy had happened to both of them but they chose to remain silent for the ride to the border. When they arrived at the border they were greeted by soldiers.

"Do you have identification?" the border guard asked as he looked at the three of them in the police car.

"He's with the Underground Railroad," Toby said. "We want to claim refugee status as American citizens escaping from slavery."

The guards came and searched them and then they went for processing. It was a long process but they were granted temporary visas but their movements would be limited until they could be granted full citizenship.

"Toby do you think maybe I can buy you a drink," Roy said as they went to one of the local bars along the border.

"What for?" Toby asked.

"To say I'm sorry," Roy said.

"Sorry for what, getting Sally and I to freedom?"

The two of them stared at each other not knowing what to say but before they knew what to say they were both hugging each other.

"Well I guess is not the United States that we knew, but I

suppose it is a free land," Roy said as he looked around to see the familiar Stars & Stripes of the American flag, albeit with fewer stars.

"Is I a free woman?" Sally said as she looked around with tears in her eyes.

"You're free," Toby said. "We are all free and living in perhaps the last free land in whatever this world that we found ourselves in."

As the three of them were standing there looking around the bar at the American Embassy that was when they saw a man approach them. He was a dark skinned African-American man dressed completely in a black trench coat that covered up most of his body. He was wearing a black hat that looked like it was from a movie from the 1940s. He had on thick black sunglasses and was smoking a thick cigar and blowing smoke in their faces.

"Excuse me that's rather rude," Roy said as he waved away the cigar smoke. "Who are you anyway?"

"Let's just say that I am a friend," the man in the trench coat said. "How would you fellas like to go home?"

Toby looked at Roy and Sally and then looked back at the man." "But we are home."

The man in the trench coat smiled. "I mean your real home. I know you fellas ain't from around here. I can send you back to where you came from, although I can't promise you that the situation is going to be better than when you left it. There will still be the same people marching with tiki torches, the same orange man in the Oval Office and all the other issues that you left behind."

"Once again who are you?" Roy asked.

"Gentlemen I'm not here to explain things to you, I'm here to ask you a simple question, would you like to go home or would you like to stay here?"

Roy and Toby looked at each other and looked at the man in the trench coat as they both nodded. "We would like to go home," they said simultaneously.

"What about Sally?" Toby asked as he ran over to Sally. "Would you like to come home with us Sally?"

"But here is my home," Sally said.

The man in the trench coat looked at them. "I think she

would find the world you came from as confusing as you found this one. But because of you she is now a free woman in a free land."

Toby wiped away a tear. "I'm going to miss you Sally. But just remember, don't let anyone ever diminish you or make you think that you are a lesser being just because of the color of your skin. You are a free woman, now and forever, and you live in a free land."

"Thank you Toby, for everything," Sally said as she kissed him.

The man in the trench coat looked at Toby and Roy.

"So what happens now?" Roy said. "How do we go home?"

"Click your heels together three times and say there is no place like home," the man in the trench coat said as he continued blowing on his cigar.

"Are you fucking kidding me?" Toby asked.

The man in the trench coat smiled as he blew smoke in both of their faces. "Yes I fucking am," he said as they both began coughing.

When the smoke cleared the man was gone and they were standing in a familiar bar where they often drank together after work.

"Are we back?" Toby asked as he ran over to a man at the bar. "Quick tell me who is president?"

"Donald Trump of course, where on earth have you been?" the man said as he shook his head.

"Sir I could kiss you," Toby said.

"So does this mean are going to vote for Trump now?" Roy asked.

"No I'm still pissed about that, but I'm happy to be home," Toby said. "God bless America, land of the free and home of the brave. I am happy to once again be in a free land."

"But only if we fight to keep it that way," Roy said with a smile as he put his arm around Toby. "Now how about that drink?"

As the two of them sat down and had their drink the man in the trench coat watched them from the back of the bar, shook his head and smiled. "Crazy niggas."

Dedicated to the protesters against bigotry and fascism at Charlottesville, especially Heather Hayes, you are all fine people, the opposition with the Tiki torches, not so much.

<u>Author Notes</u>

I conceived of this story shortly after the events of Charlottesville. I already had plenty of ideas involving alternate history stories where the Confederacy won the Civil War or where the Nazis won World War II, as those are pretty much the most popular scenarios for alternate history, and I thought that it would be interesting to combine them. But I also wanted to make it more directly relevant to the events of Charlottesville itself specifically.

I thought of the idea for this in September 2017 and started writing the first three or four chapters in November 2017 intending to finish it while it was immediately relevant, but then for whatever reason I guess I just forgot about it and never got around to finishing it. I kept meaning to get back to it eventually but for whatever reason I didn't get back to it until later in 2019, where I think it only grew in relevance during that stretch of time and I think that that was to the benefit of the story overall.

I knew that the country was already heading down a bad path as soon as Donald Trump made his appearance on the scene but I didn't want this story to be a specifically anti-Trump story, even though that is the main commentary. I wanted to be more about racism in general and the racism that sparked the events of Charlottesville. That was when I think that most sane people in the nation started to realize that the racial conflicts were getting a lot worse under this current administration and just getting out of hand. When it's safer in this country for Nazis to march around with tiki torches chanting "Jews will not replace us" than it is for a black man to kneel at a football game you know that our nation is definitely on the wrong track, very far on the wrong track.

The framing device that I thought of for this story was inspired by what sparked the protests of Charlottesville in the first place; the desire to remove racist symbols of the Confederacy that many people think is a part of their heritage that they want to celebrate. So I thought that it would be interesting to have two police officers, one white and proud of his Southern heritage, and one black who experiences the direct racist implications of such symbols and what they mean. The conflict in the first chapter establishes their different attitudes which they both find to be challenged when they find themselves in a much more awful world, but a world that is in many ways a mirror of our own.

The purpose of this story was of course directly a dystopian satire involving alternate history. How much a different timeline would resemble ours at all is very difficult to say. It probably wouldn't closely resemble our world at all, but to some degree you just have to try to frame it according to what you know happened afterwards. So when I worked out the alternate history of this timeline that they find themselves on I tried to think of which course history would take if the Confederacy had won the Civil War and the ramifications that that would have on world history and not just United States history.

There are many who feel that slavery would have inevitably collapsed in the South as industrialization came by, but at the same time I am not quite sure. Given that the civil rights movement only happened relatively recently in our history and there are still many people alive who remember a time when segregation was a fact, we can only imagine how much more it would be delayed in a Confederate state. In a Confederate state it may be very well possible that slavery, as backward as an institution as it is, could very well continue to the present day.

How this would affect the rest of world history is difficult to say. I figure that a northern defeat would result in the union states sort of shirking from the scene. The defeat would probably demoralize them and they would reluctantly have to let the southern states go. It is my belief that if the North was its own independent nation it would probably continue along more progressive lines than the South, but with the nation split apart they would follow very distinctly different paths. The Confederacy, being the victor in the war, would likely be the one who ended up expanding westward and conquering the West and likely more brutally, while the North would probably end up being a more minor power and would probably not grow into a superpower the way the United States did in our history.

In this timeline I give the Confederacy perhaps more credit than it deserves. Would it have gone on to conquer most of the West as well as parts of Mexico and South America? It's difficult to say, but for the purposes of this story I figured that it would be the Confederacy in the ascendancy while the North would go on decline.

Now if we think about how world history plays out it's not that hard of a stretch to imagine that something like the rise of Nazi Germany still could happen. It is very likely if the United States was two separate countries they might not get involved in World War I or they would take separate sides, so the outcome of World War I that led to the rise of Nazi Germany might very well not have happened. But again for the purposes of this story, in order to allow me to imagine the worst of all possible worlds, I imagine the Confederacy supporting the axis powers who ultimately gained a victory and who share a mutual alliance based on their desire for white supremacy of the world.

This would ultimately leave the northern United States, or just the United States, as sort of a small outpost of freedom in a world that is overrun by authoritarian, racist and totalitarian states that have a mutual alliance. So the North ultimately becomes the free land of the title that everybody wants to escape to.

I also thought about how technology might progress and how that would help or hinder the development of slavery. Assuming that institution of slavery continued you would have to assume that modern technology would be used to reinforce that system. So we could very well imagine a world where the Confederacy became some type of a racist theocracy and developed technology to track slaves and to make it more difficult for them to resist. Once again it's hard to know whether slavery would still continue into the 21st century, but given that slavery still exists in many parts of the world, and by some accounts there are more slaves in the world today than at any point in history, it's not that far-fetched to believe that a Confederate States of America could maintain a system of slavery even well into the 21st century.

Beyond that though any type of world is basically possible once you begin to speculate, but you want to make the world kind of familiar, and for the purposes of satire I made the horrible Confederate world to be a place where a lot of people in the South who still waive Confederate flags 150 years later and still haven't gotten over the loss of the Civil War, would be very much at home in this alternate timeline. Things like the border wall, nigger lives matter, make the Confederacy great again and all these things are of course direct references to our world to put things in perspective, so perhaps be a little more suspension of disbelief, but I think that this world does genuinely parallel our world in many ways.

The ultimate lesson was for the two characters to examine their own views and attitudes in light of a world that is much worse. The whole purpose of satire is to exaggerate and this is something of an exaggerated dystopia, but I do imagine that the world would be quite a horrible place if these events actually did happen. In a world where the Confederacy and the Nazis were triumphant it's easy to imagine an entire world that comes under the domination of white supremacy, which even in the modern world on this timeline is unfortunately on the rise.

I suppose each character has sort of a different character arc. Roy is made to confront his own racism by seeing it play out more in the extreme. Never considering himself a bigot when he finds himself on this truly terrible world who realizes just how prevailing racism is on the world that he originally came from.

Toby's arc is more about trying to fight for his own freedom in a world where he was born without the advantages he had in this world.

Both of them eventually realize that our world may not be perfect but for all its imperfections is still not the worst possible world. But it also makes them want to fight to improve to make sure that our world doesn't end up resembling that other world that they found themselves in.

I'll admit that I didn't really put much in the way of explanation for how or why things happened but there is sort of an Easter egg in this story that is my attempt to create a shared universe. For fans of my previous novel, Day of Infamy, you may very well recognize the nameless mysterious man in black in the trench coat who is sort of the facilitator of interdimensional travel and parallel timelines. So although I don't explain it in much detail, if you have read Day of Infamy you would get the reference that he is a facilitator of interdimensional travel between parallel timelines. I have no doubt that he will appear in many more future novels and novellas because I find that alternate history and alternate timelines are one of my favorite topics.

I also don't doubt that I will have future books set in dystopian worlds similar to this one. Once you start contemplating all the different ways that history can play out and how much worse things can possibly be the possibilities are endless. So I consider this only the first of what will probably be a lifetime of writing stories about horrible worlds where the Confederacy and Nazis have made things so much worse. But in the meantime I hope that for a first novel addressing these questions that this was a good first attempt and I hope that you enjoyed it and look forward to more similar stories in the future.

Let us all keep fighting to make this world a better place so that it does not become the world displayed in this story. We must never forget the lessons that came at Charlottesville and that I think that unfortunately we still have a very long way to go before we are fully able to overcome the darker aspects of our society and our history.

For more samples of my writing check out my blog at https://stephensipila.wordpress.com/ and follow me on twitter at https://twitter.com/StephenSipila.
Stephen Sipila
2/10/20